If you could shift into a wolf, what would you discover about yourself?

Two years after the deaths of her bond mates, Constance Newcastle is ready to start over. The problem? The rest of the Great Pack, gathered in Paris to shift into wolves together, is not so sure she deserves the chance. Although the Great Council ruled the car crash an accident, even Constance blames herself. She was driving, after all.

Treated like a pariah by those she longs to rejoin, Constance reunites with an old lover. Everything looks promising until he mysteriously dies. Accused of his murder and desperate to clear her name, Constance joins forces with handsome, confident Liam Murphy, a former Alpha pack leader with a past as tragic and troubled as her own. Guided by the mysterious Councilor Jason Allerton, Constance and Liam discover they are not alone-- throughout the Great Pack, people are dying. Can all the deaths be accidents, or is something more sinister going on?

Books by Amy Lee Burgess

The Wiolf Within Series
Beneath the Skin, Book One
Scratch the Surface, Book Two
Hidden In Plain Sight, Book Three
Inside Out, Book Four
About Face, Book Five
Across the Line, Book Six

Published by Kensington Publishing Corporation

Beneath the Skin

The Wolf Within Series

Amy Lee Burgess

LYRICAL PRESS
Kensington Publishing Corp.
www.kensingtonbooks.com

Lyrical Press books are published by
Kensington Publishing Corp. 119 West 40th Street New York, NY 10018

All Kensington titles, imprints, and distributed lines are available at special
quantity discounts for bulk purchases for sales promotion, premiums, fund-
raising, and educational or institutional use.

Special book excerpts or customized printings can also be created to fit
specific needs. For details, write or phone the office of the Kensington
Special Sales Manager:
Kensington Publishing Corp.
119 West 40th Street
New York, NY 10018
Attn. Special Sales Department. Phone: 1-800-221-2647.

First Electronic Edition: October 2011
eISBN-13: 978-1-61650-323-9
eISBN-10: 1-61650-323-8

First Print Edition: October 2011
ISBN-13: 1-61650-852-3
ISBN-10: 1-61650-852-3

Printed in the United States of America

Before I ever took the first scary step toward submitting this novel for publication, I spent several years sharing my writing with a core group of friends without whom I wouldn't have had the courage to reach further. My eternal gratitude to all of you--Kim Murphy, Chris Wilbanks, Portia Scott Palko, Michelle Guillory and Elizabeth Myrddin--you have no idea how much your support has meant to me.

I'd also like to dedicate this novel to Nerine Dorman for her constant inspiration and encouragement.

And, Michael, this novel wouldn't be here if you hadn't challenged me to do NaNoWriMo last year.

Chapter 1

Run. Run, run, run. Scared. Littles hide, no scrape legs, no make noise. Wind no push things. Fur stick up. Me scared. Me follow scent. Her. Me love Her. See big hard thing. Pushed in. Black water drip, drip, drip. Blood. Smell blood. Drip, drip, drip. Scared. See Her. See Her in big hard thing. Her two legs now. Her eyes no see Me. Look up to Big Shiny and little shinies. No see. Smell blood. Smell Her. No hear beat thing. No hear blood move under skin. Her no move no more. Her gone. Me look up see Big Shiny. Me cry loud.

* * * *

When I jerked awake, a smothered scream on my lips, the digital clock on the nightstand read five thirty-two in the morning. I rolled over and reached out instinctively for the reassuring warmth of Grey's body, but of course he wasn't there. He never would be there again.

Two years, I told myself as I threw back the covers of the single bed in a small, unfamiliar Paris hotel room and staggered for the bathroom to splash cold water on my face. The dregs of the dream slipped away under my fingertips as I massaged my cheeks and forehead, blond hair spilling over my shoulders into the wet stream of the water.

My hair was getting long. *Two years*, I told myself again, bitterness twisting my face.

I scowled into the mirror and saw my own reflection—as familiar to me as anything in the world. I thought of the wind, the trees at night, the scent of the pine needles embedded in the soft earth of the forest.

Everything conspired to create a wall between me and the rest of the world. I hadn't connected with anything or anyone for so long I barely remembered what it felt like not to be alone.

My thirty-second birthday had come and gone three months earlier. Once upon a time there would have been a celebration. Grey and Elena would have been there with me. Presents. Cake.

Instead I'd sat in a dark theater and watched a horror movie while secretly envying all the couples who sat around me.

When I saw people in love, a strange, isolating ache gripped my whole body.

Two years, I told my reflection in the mirror.

Grey used to tell me I was beautiful. He loved to trace the contours of my face with his fingers—my high cheekbones, my full mouth, my eyelids and forehead. Even my nose, which I thought was too big but he pronounced elegant. Ha.

He was the elegant one with his sensitive mouth and long, thin fingers. A poet's face. Hollow cheeks, dreamy eyes.

Elena had been the beauty in my opinion. Blond, like me, only hers was so fair it was nearly white. The milky translucence of her skin made me think of women in castles in the medieval days, women who stayed behind the castle walls and never saw the sun because of the feuds and fights their men waged for them.

Grey and Elena—my bond mates, my lovers, my friends.

There had also been Jonathan, Nora, Callie, Vaughn and Peter. Grandfather Tobias. My pack.

Two years ago, that is.

When everything stopped.

* * * *

I spent the day shopping. I ended up at Au Printemps on the boulevard Haussman where I sorted through a bewildering array of bright, modern dresses and used my limited French with the saleswoman who tried to steer me away from black toward something brighter.

"*Tout le monde préfère des robes noires, mais, pour vous, madame, je pense rouge! Voila!*" She produced a shimmering red gown with a plunging sequined neckline and a nearly indecent slit up the right thigh.

I had thought something a little plainer. Something that would allow me to blend into the background, because I wasn't sure I wanted attention.

Two years, I heard my own accusing voice say in my head then, abruptly, I agreed to try on the dress. If I didn't like it, I would stick with the original plan.

Ten seconds after staring at my reflection in the three-way mirror in the dressing room, I abandoned my idea of blending into the background. I looked gorgeous. Gorgeous, hell. I hadn't even felt pretty in so long. The crimson color made my blond hair glow and darkened my eyes to navy. I looked regal and self-assured. It was a dress that would force people to take me seriously. For two years I'd felt invisible. In this red dress that would be impossible.

Of course it wasn't cheap and I winced at the hit on my bank balance as I paid. Back in my little hotel room I had a new pair of fantastic cherry red stiletto pumps that would be the perfect accompaniment. Paris was proving to be an expensive adventure.

As I left, the saleswoman wished me a good afternoon, and that she hoped I would enjoy myself at the party tonight.

Party. I nearly snorted aloud at the idea. It was a not a party. No one there would dream to call it something as frivolous as that, even if there would be canapés and cocktails, three or four different types of music, candles and designer clothes. People there would laugh and flirt, dance and drink, but it was not a party.

It was a gathering. The Great Gathering.

So many of the Great Pack would be there from all over the world, maybe including people I hadn't seen in five years, since before Grey and Elena had died.

There I would be in a bold, sexy red dress without them, and everyone would see me. My stomach lurched. What was I thinking?

I turned around on the sidewalk so I could return the dress. I should be in mourning still. I should wear black. What kind of a message would I send with a red dress? Could I afford that message? After all, everyone thought—my own former pack even—it was my fault they were dead— Elena and Grey. Of course I thought so too.

After all, I had driven the car that night.

My pack's eyes had been so cold when they'd severed ties with me. Jonathan's, especially. He was Alpha, the leader, but Grey had been a favorite in the pack, even if he hadn't been Alpha. He could have been, but he didn't want to. He said no when Vaughn asked. Everyone had been a little shocked he'd turned it down. After all, everyone wanted to be Alpha at some point in their lives. But then he explained it to me. Some people needed to lead more than others, and that popularity didn't prove the best indicator of need. Jonathan needed to lead. If he'd been under another male, he would have chafed at it, and the bonds between us all would have suffered. Besides, Alphas rotated. We'd get our chance. Let Jonathan go first. Grey had been so wise. So good. He would have made a much better Alpha than Jonathan, and now he would never have the chance.

It was November in Paris and cold even with the wintry sunlight filtering down through the clouds. A gust of wind rattled the plastic bag in my hand and blew the skirt of a tall woman who walked in front of me. She squealed a little, and held it down while her companion laughed indulgently beside her and said something in rapid-fire French.

The sun struck her hair and lit it up into a white-gold halo around her head and, for a moment, I thought of Elena. The sun used to turn her hair into a white-gold halo too sometimes.

My heart hurt so badly inside my chest I couldn't breathe, and I stopped dead on the sidewalk and squeezed my eyes shut against the sudden blinding burn of tears.

Two years. When would it ever stop? When could I walk down the street and see the sun hit some woman's hair and not be overcome with grief? When could I wake from a nightmare and stop reaching out for somebody who wasn't there?

When would I run through the forest on all fours, fur whipping back against the wind, knowing I was with my bond mates, safe and secure, and above all, loved?

Even though my hotel was only a few streets away, I didn't feel like walking. Yet I wanted to escape the Paris afternoon where everyone was happy and be alone with my thoughts of dead connections.

Instead I found a sidewalk café and ordered hot chocolate. I sat on the cold wrought-iron chair in the Paris sunshine and shivered a little in my navy blue pea coat as I people-watched until my drink arrived.

It was sweet and warm, and I tried to convince myself I deserved to live again and to be happy. Over the past two years, I'd paid my dues to the Great Pack, to everyone, and tonight was my chance to start over again. I was not the same as I once was, but I could start over again. The invitation to the Great Gathering proved it, even though it was my right to attend, because the two years had been up three months ago, on my birthday.

The clock always reset on birthdays. It was a day to examine yourself and your ties and bonds, to renew them if you wanted or dissolve them, if you could. At least start the process if it wasn't a mutual agreement.

My pack had severed our ties on Jonathan's birthday. It was the first pack birthday after the accident and they only waited that long because they had to. The accident had occurred on the night of my birthday, and by the time they all knew about it and the circumstances surrounding it, it was already past midnight and the chance to dissolve then had passed.

They'd formally severed ties on Jonathan's birthday, because that was how our laws worked. They'd blamed me for the accident, and instead of offering me comfort, they'd condemned me.

I hadn't protested back then. I was too shocked—too shattered by the knowledge Grey and Elena were gone. I had felt guilty because I had been driving and it had been my idea to go to the club that night. Why shouldn't we have gone out? It was my birthday. I was young and happy and I loved to dance. So why shouldn't I have wanted to go to a dance club?

I saw their hostile faces as I had been interrogated by the Councils at my tribunal, after they'd had time to think about it and talk about it among themselves without me. I smelled them too and I knew. They smelled of the same despair and grief I gave off. But they also smelled of anger—against me.

One thing about being Pack, we could smell emotions. We could try to mask our feelings from each other, but our scents usually gave us away.

Others, people who weren't Pack, couldn't do this. It was one of the things, besides shape-shifting, that made us different.

All my life it had been drilled into me that the Others would not understand our kind. We would be persecuted and bullied, isolated and studied. Perhaps even exterminated. I was kept away, home schooled when I was little. The only people I knew until I was eight or nine years old were the members of my birth pack.

One day my mother brought me to a grocery store. All the Others scared me, I remember that. A world that had consisted of twenty-four people who were Pack had suddenly changed and twisted. My insular little existence had been shattered, and the idea of the Others scared me. They outnumbered us. They always had, they always would. Somehow we had to coexist. We could know about them, but they could never know about us.

My father made me watch werewolf movies so I would understand that I needed to keep silent about what I really was. I didn't like the way those movies made me feel. Hunted, persecuted. I wasn't a bit like any of the monsters in any of the movies or books, but he told me the Others would not see the difference.

We had no special protection in wolf form. We didn't bite people, or change them into wolves like us. We didn't even call it *werewolf*. We called it being Pack. You had to be born Pack, or you would never be Pack.

The legends of being bitten by a werewolf then turning into one were just that—legends. The grandmothers and grandfathers said the legends protected us. Spread false information about something real and you could hide behind the legends. Twist it just enough so no one would believe you, even if you told them the truth. Not that we would. Who would believe, and what profit would come of it if they did?

Some of the Pack, especially the older ones, thought my generation was soft and the ones after us only getting softer. We were losing touch with our beast natures and becoming weak. We used our ability to shape shift as if it were a hobby, as if we were in a secret club. Our nature no longer defined us and gave us strength and purpose of will. Or so the grandfathers and grandmothers said.

I supposed modern life had made things easier. I'm not sure about softer. In the modern world it was harder to disguise the fact we aged much slower than Others. We lived in isolated areas. Switched jobs often, changed social security numbers and passports. Of course most of the grandfathers and grandmothers disdained such things. They usually lived under the radar. They preferred not to have *Other* identities. They might live in cities but they didn't vote or own businesses. They did nothing but exist on the fringe. If they traveled, they paid cash and used transportation that didn't require ID. Or, if they still were up for it, they traveled in shifted form.

They had jobs, but menial labor, under the table. Or they stole, begged or borrowed.

Most Pack members were particularly adept at pick-pocketing and sleight of hand. Lots of the grandfathers and grandmothers gambled for a living. They ran shell games or dice or any game of chance.

The younger generation liked material comforts. We didn't want to live in squalor, or squat illegally on somebody else's property, or rely on someone "legit" in our pack to provide us with housing. Lots of the old grandfathers and grandmothers lived in homes owned by their children and grandchildren.

Since we weren't the Alpha couple in our pack, Grey and I hadn't been allowed to have children. In the old days, if you got pregnant and you weren't Alpha that meant going to an old grandmother for a potion to miscarry. Nowadays we had modern birth control, thankfully. Not that the old grandmothers endorsed such things. They had herbal concoctions but their efficacy was not as reliable as the Pill.

The old ways were good enough for us, they lectured. They should be good enough for you. But why not use something better if it was available?

That's how I thought anyway.

Chapter 2

Registration for the Great Gathering began at seven o'clock. One of the Paris packs owned a large chateau about an hour outside the city. Chartered buses had been set up to ferry those of us not privileged enough to rate lodging there back and forth to the city.

At 5:45 PM I boarded one of these buses, hoping I wouldn't see anyone I knew. I wasn't ready yet. My heart pounded like hell against my ribcage, and one moment I burned up, then a minute later I froze. Tears choked me so I could barely breathe.

I was bundled up against the Paris cold in my best wool coat, a pair of leather gloves and a purple scarf wound around and around my neck. Nobody could see my jewelry then work out for themselves that I was unbonded.

I supposed they could see me sitting by myself and figure it out, but sometimes packs sent representatives if they couldn't afford for all to attend.

The bus seated fifty people. I was the fourth one on and took a window seat in the middle. I craned my neck as I looked out and tried to give the impression I waited for someone, maybe my bond mate or a pack mate, to join me.

But I bet my smell was all wrong. I bet I exuded a mixture of trepidation, shame and desire.

Nobody sat by me for the longest time. It wasn't until the bus driver shouted out the door in French that there was room for one more that I finally got a seat mate.

A teenage girl with mousy brown hair and a petulant expression slumped into the seat next to me. She spent the entire drive examining her black nail polish and popping her gum and studiously ignoring me. She didn't want to be beside me anymore than I wanted to be beside her.

If I smelled, she didn't react to it.

She was so young this had to be her first Great Gathering. Teenagers fifteen to nineteen were allowed to attend. Instead of mixing with the adults, they stayed together in a conference room of their own with one or two grandmothers or grandfathers as chaperones. Field trips and events were organized. Sometimes they found future bond mates, but most of the time they either brooded sullenly or played games. Nowadays it was Wii or Nintendo. Back in the days of the grandfathers and grandmothers it had been board games.

When I had been sixteen, I'd attended a Regional Gathering in upper state New York.

"You can make a living off chess," I remembered the old grandfather growling at us, his teen charges. "When I was Alpha, I supported my whole pack by playing chess against Others in the park. You can't do that with these damn electronic games. Only thing they're good for is making you go blind and ruining your hearing. Damn shame, if you ask me."

We hadn't told the grandfather that plenty of our generation made lots of money gaming online and at clubs and arcades. He wouldn't have understood and, even if he had, he would have condemned it as against the old ways.

An Other lifespan is about seventy-five years give or take. Those of us who are Pack live about one hundred and fifty. We age normally until we hit our twenties, where we seem to stall for years and years. The last fifty years or so we look old, but never older than a normal sixty or sixty-five year old. We die of normal diseases and, if we're autopsied by Others, which is rare considering packs take care of their own dead, we don't appear any different inside. I suppose if the right blood analysis was performed they might detect some anomalies, but the right tests are never performed, because there is no need for them. It would have to be an accidental discovery. Our blood would need to be mixed with the proper distilled herbs, and why would anyone do that?

Even without living under the radar, we lived under the radar.

* * * *

Outside my bus window the Paris skyline gave way to the French countryside. It all passed in a blur. I'd only been to one Great Gathering in my life when I was eighteen. This would be the first time I would mingle with the group at large. I'd never attended a Gathering alone. For the past two years, I'd existed in a twilight excess of Others, deliberately exiled from my own kind. I didn't know if I even remembered how to talk to someone Pack. I felt rusty and conspicuous as if everyone would know my past, even though they couldn't possibly. Odds were I wouldn't see even one person I knew. New England packs were notoriously clannish and parsimonious. Not many of them would spend the money to travel to Paris, especially since there were so many Regionals in the area. Keyed up and nervous, I was as cold on the outside as I was on the inside. My legs had goose bumps, because I wasn't wearing stockings with the dress and my coat didn't come down as long as the gown.

The girl beside me was dressed in designer jeans and Ugg boots, a fashionable parka—fuchsia and turquoise. Loud as hell, and it hurt my eyes even under the muted reading lights.

The entire ride she texted, probably to someone in the bus immediately before or behind us.

As I looked at her, I couldn't remember ever being so young.

When I was twenty and he was twenty-two, Grey and I had bonded. Elena had joined with us at a Regional Gathering two years after that. We'd both loved Elena. She'd completed us almost from the first night we met her.

Packs were made up of duos and triads. There were no adult singles. If someone from a duo died, the one left behind either bonded with another duo in the pack, found someone from a different pack, or the ties were severed. The only exception was with elders of at least a hundred years old. They had an honorary position in the pack at best by that point and were allowed to affiliate, but they usually only socialized. They were supported by the pack so they always had a place to live and food to eat. It was like Pack social security. You contributed all your life and paid your dues to your pack. When you were too old to participate and contribute, your pack took care of you based on what you did for them. It was a good system for the most part.

The older you got, the harder it was to shape shift. I think it's because shape-shifting is tied to sex. That got harder as people aged too. People could still do it, but most of the time the desire was not there anymore.

The grandfathers and grandmothers loved to lecture us, but I thought they were the ones who had lost touch with what it meant to be Pack. When was the last time they'd ever shifted? You heard stories of virile grandfathers and seductive grandmothers who managed to attract and seduce someone younger in the pack, but for some of them it had been decades since they'd shifted, even if they had bond mates.

The wheels of the bus crunched loudly down a gravel driveway leading to an imposing white chateau topped with a slate blue roof. Lost in my private reveries, I had been taken by surprise when we left the smooth road for the gravel drive. I had to scramble to minimize the sudden assault of sound. Pack had a dimmer switch sort of control over our senses that we dialed up or down as we concentrated. Some of us were set higher or lower, it just depended. I was one of the ones who was higher, even in human form.

I'd learned to dial way down out of self-preservation. It had been a hard-won lesson. The first time I'd shifted I'd spent the entire time trying to escape this awful, huge booming sound. Like a bass drum only more organic. It wasn't until I'd shifted back that I'd realized it was my own damn heart that had driven me crazy.

I had been eighteen, and for those of us who were close to twenty, the age of Pack majority, it really chafed that we weren't yet allowed to participate fully in the Great Gathering. We'd disdained the younger teens and the grandmother left to chaperone us and instead spent our time drinking and smoking pot behind the plantation home in Louisiana where the Gathering had taken place. Heavy petting had been pretty much demanded if you'd wanted to be even marginally cool.

It had only been a short skip from that to actual sex.

Something happened when two people who were Pack had sex. There was an exchange of essence, something indefinable that created the energy you needed to shift. You didn't have to do it every time you had sex, and you didn't have to shift right after it. Usually there was a twenty-four to forty-eight hour window and you could shift at any point during that time. You got better and had greater control over this the more you shifted.

Once I talked to a grandmother in my pack about sex and shifting. I thought it was magical, this exchange of essence. She laughed at me, yes, it was, but it was more than the exchange of essence, it was the exchange of fluid too.

"Saliva, sweat and semen, child, sharing that is just as essential as this magical essence you can't see."

We never used condoms with each other, and I guess that's part of the reason. We needed to exchange fluids.

One of the boys in our teen group at that Great Gathering when I was eighteen proposed a dare—that we stage our own Great Hunt, to hell with the adults. We could screw, shift, then hunt in the sugar cane fields behind the plantation.

My partner was a young German boy two days older than me. He spoke very little English, but man, could he kiss. I still dreamed sometimes about his kisses. Slow and urgent, fueled by teen passion, sexy because we could barely communicate with words. Instead of using our mouths to talk, we used them to kiss. That's how we talked, that German boy and I.

We broke the rules when we shifted, of course. When you first shifted, you were supposed to be initiated by an experienced member of your Pack. You usually got to choose who, but they were free to decline the invitation. People rarely did, because it was considered an honor to be chosen as someone's mentor. Once you got the hang of it, you were encouraged to find a bond mate. If you didn't find one within a few years, one was generally found for you.

There were always a few who never bonded, but there was usually something wrong with them. After they turned twenty-six they lost their privileges and kept to the fringes of their birth packs where they were looked after but never treated as equals. Some people turned their backs on the Great Pack and lived in the world of the Others. They denied their wolves and who they really were. Most of the time these were people who'd lost their bond mate and didn't want another. Some of them, like me, had been exiled for some transgression or crime they'd committed. Those exiled had to exist on their own for two years before they could even attempt to find a new pack. When they did return, everything was forgiven and the slate was wiped clean. In theory. In practice, some people kept score and judged. I supposed that was only natural, but I was determined to keep my past exile a secret at this Great Gathering if I could help it. I knew I'd have to tell some people, but the whole damn Pack didn't need to know.

* * * *

A set of stone stairs led up to the massive front doors of the chateau. They were thrown open and light spilled out into the courtyard from a large reception hall. Skirted tables were set up along the walls manned by mostly women with laptops who searched for names in the database. When they found the right one, they clicked a few keys and a nametag spat out of a printer next to them.

The nametag contained the person's name and their pack, as well as their country of origin.

It stuck with adhesive to clothing, for which I was grateful. No pins to ruin my new expensive French gown.

When I pasted my nametag on my chest, I felt exposed because all it said was *Constance Newcastle—Boston, Massachusetts, USA.*

Of course my jewelry also proclaimed me as unbonded and unaffiliated with a pack.

To indicate mated status, everyone wore pendants with different colored stones in them. Birthstones—one stone for the unbonded, two for a duo, three for a triad.

My pendant was a simple peridot suspended by a silver chain.

Pack membership jewelry differed. Bracelets, rings, necklaces: they were distinctive and designed by the pack. It wasn't hard to spot a piece of pack jewelry, but it wasn't as specific as a mating status pendant.

It was hot in the chateau with the press of bodies, and I took off my coat somewhat awkwardly, trying to balance it and my purse and not bash anyone in the face with a flailing arm.

Distinctive laughter rang out and I spun on my heel. I knew that laugh. It was Callie, from my old pack. Peter and Vaughn flanked her protectively. Peter pretended to cop a feel as he stuck Callie's nametag on her dress. He was always the jokester, Peter.

I smiled to see them and warmth stole through my body. I suddenly felt at home. I had been alone for two years, and seeing them now made those years disappear somehow.

"Callie!" I called and the three of them looked at me. All the laughter and fun died out of their faces. Callie took Vaughn's hand and tugged him away. Peter followed, his gaze the last to leave mine. They turned their backs on me, shunning me, and disappeared into the crowd

Someone near me laughed. I don't suppose they laughed at me. No one paid particular attention to me, but that laugh cut through me like a sword, sliced me open, exposed all my weaknesses and vulnerabilities.

Ashamed, I pushed against the tide of the crowd and forced my way back onto the stone steps only to see the last of the buses pulling away. The first departure was not until midnight. By my watch, it was barely seven o'clock. For a moment, I observed people as they flowed up the staircase and inside the chateau. They all seemed to arrive in pairs or groups. Search as I would, I couldn't find anybody on their own. I imagined stories for them as they passed by without even seeing me. All the stories were happy because everyone smiled. It was a Great Gathering. Alliances would be forged, friendships renewed, memories made.

Of course I couldn't achieve any of those things if I stood all night long on the front steps and waited for the damn bus to come back.

Back inside I let the crowd direct me to a winding staircase that I followed up a level. The entire second floor of this particular wing of the chateau was a ballroom. An intricate floor made of blocks and strips of wood had been inlaid with painstaking precision by hand. Eight massive crystal chandeliers hung suspended like glittering ice from the ceiling that was painted with a series of frescos of men, women and wolves, all intertwined and frolicking together. Some of the people looked half wolf, some of the wolves half human.

I could have looked at the ceiling for hours, but I couldn't stand there with my head tilted back like a dolt, gaping, so I found a seat at a large round table in the corner of the room, a table that was not prominent and reserved, as were several of them—the ones near the front.

A huge head table had been placed just before a series of arching floor-to-ceiling windows—for the Council and their bond mates.

The Great Council comprised the crème de la crème of the Great Pack. Members of the Council were all past Alphas of their packs. Theirs were influential ones.

Councilors chose Advisors. Advisors were the record-keepers of the Great Pack, the guardians of our knowledge, our numbers, our secrets and our past. Many Councilors were once Advisors.

In conjunction with the Regional Councils, the Great Council oversaw disputes and investigated accidents and murders. They sent Advisors in first to gather the facts before the Councilors made a ruling.

The seats on the Council fluctuated with our population. Councilors on the Great Council generally had two or three Advisors—whereas Councilors on the Regionals normally only had one.

We were taught to both respect and fear the Councils, especially the Great. Most of us were mainly in awe of it.

The head table was set for at least fifty tonight, which meant about twenty-five Councilors were in attendance. A good turn-out, but then, this was a Great Gathering.

Beyond the windows was a decorative pond with several splashing fountains lit up in pink, green, blue, purple and gold.

Tablecloths of dark gold adorned each table. Chairs were wrapped in gold and plum fabric tied back with broad ribbons. Dark purple goblets and matching napkins folded into intricate shapes marked each place setting.

It was gorgeous and very French.

I draped my coat over the back of one of the gold chairs and sat so I faced the windows and fountains, my back to most of the room.

I had this ridiculous urge to start crying, because everybody in the room had somebody else to be with and I didn't. Who else my age didn't have a pack or a bond mate? What if I were the only one? I was supposed to be there to find a bond mate and new pack, but what if there were no one who wanted me? I'd been lonely on my own, but this gnawing, horrible feeling of inferiority and worthlessness was worse than the loneliest night I'd spent in Boston. Which was stupid, because I'd been waiting so long for this chance. Sure, at first after Grey and Elena died and Riverglow had turned against me, I'd sworn I'd never belong to another pack. But that was at first when my grief and betrayal both burned so hot and high I didn't have time to be wistful.

Lately, wistful was pretty much all I ever felt. I wanted to belong again.

I had nothing to be ashamed of. My pack may have blamed me for the deaths of Grey and Elena, but the Councils had not.

They'd sent one of the American Great Councilors to our pack in Connecticut, and after he had heard all the evidence and my story of what had happened, he and the Regional Council cleared me of all culpability. My pack still severed ties with me. I could have been taken into Jonathan and Nora's duo and we could have made a triad, but they had not even considered the idea.

Tonight the wistfulness was accompanied by guilt. Was I really here to replace Grey and Elena? Just so I wouldn't be alone? But I wouldn't ever forget them. How could I? Was it a crime to move on? Is that why I felt so guilty?

Instead of dwelling on my guilt, I focused on the sights and scents around me.

Music was piped into the room through strategically placed speakers. At the moment, it was American pop, but later in the evening it would change to something fast and danceable.

The tables were arranged so a huge space for dancing remained. At the moment, tables piled with cheese, fruit and sliced meat, as well as savory things wrapped in pastry and baked until light golden brown, filled this space. The food smelled divine and I realized I hadn't eaten since breakfast.

I fixed myself a heaping plate of almost everything and, with a crystal glass of champagne I'd snatched from a white-coated waiter bearing a full tray, I retreated to my table.

It was one with seating enough for ten. During my absence, a duo with twin teenage boys had taken seats near mine. The woman was dark-haired and, although she looked to be around twenty-five or thirty, she was probably closer to fifty. Her bond mate was about the same age with untidy brown hair and a look of being perpetually dismayed by the things his offspring chose to do and say.

The twins looked no older than sixteen. Tall and gangly with the same untidy brown hair as their father but with their mother's cool, gray eyes, they openly ogled me as I sat. Well, I couldn't blame them. My cleavage was very much on display.

One of them nudged the other hard with his elbow, so his brother dipped his fingers in his glass and flicked the water at his twin who then retaliated.

Their mother removed the plate of food between them adroitly and their father looked as if he wanted to pretend he didn't know them.

"Forgive their rambunctiousness, please," he said. His accent was Australian, although I'd picked that up from his nametag. His name was Evan. His bond mate was Deb and his sons were Max and Matthew. They were from a pack called Moonglen. I'd never heard of it.

The parents peered blatantly at my pendant. Evan's eyes widened in surprise, while Deb's mouth tightened.

"I think the singles tables are over there." She pointed imperiously toward the other side of the room where a group of early twenty-somethings laughed.

I was only thirty-two, but I felt a lifetime older than them. I had experience as a contributing pack member, as a bond mate in both a duo and a triad. If they were still single, chances are they'd never been outside their own packs save for perhaps a few Gatherings, most likely Regionals.

They knew nothing compared to me.

But I picked up my glass and plate then had to set them down again to get my coat and purse. In the end I abandoned the champagne and walked away.

I heard Evan remonstrating Deb and she gave a sharp reply that shut him up. As I walked away, I could feel the twins' gazes as they ogled my ass as I walked.

The twenty-somethings fell silent at my approach, and two of the men eyed me appreciatively.

The prettiest woman at the table scrutinized my name tag. When she saw I didn't have a pack she knew I had to be at least twenty-six years old. At twenty-six, unbonded people lost all their birth pack rights.

"You're kind of old for us." She tossed her glossy blond hair and the two men who sized me up were suddenly captivated by her. The name tag on her low-cut blue halter dress read *Tora Nilsson, Frostpaw, Lund, Sweden*. She pointed vaguely in the direction of yet another table then turned her back as if I did not even exist.

Funny how I hadn't wanted to sit with them, because I thought they were too young and inexperienced, yet rejection made my cheeks sting. For a bitter moment, I wished I'd stayed in Boston, screw this, but then my better sense reasserted itself. Of course this wasn't going to be easy. Nothing ever was.

I sat at my third table and decided I wasn't going to move again. To hell with anyone who said anything. My food wouldn't stay warm forever and I was hungry.

The people at this table didn't say anything when I settled. They hadn't said much of anything before I took my seat. There were three woman and two men. They all reeked of frustration and anger. Great. I had blundered into a table full of fighting pack mates. I kept my gaze on my plate and ate everything. I was starving.

"Constance, my dear, how wonderful to see you!" A man's voice broke into my reverie. I looked up, hoping I didn't have crumbs stuck to my lipstick, and almost died.

Jason Allerton stood beside the table. Councilor Jason Allerton. Handsome, rich, polished and smooth—the man from the Great Council who had cleared me after the accident.

"Why don't you come have a drink with me?" Councilor Allerton hovered his hand at the small of my back, not quite touching me, and with the power of his voice and presence, led me to the bar in the back of the room.

"You certainly can't sit there," he told me as if he cared one way or the other. "There's a table up front where I'd like you to sit. I want you to meet someone."

I was instantly suspicious but also intrigued.

He snapped his fingers at the bartender who leaped over to us. Everyone responded to Allerton's powerful aura, even the Others.

Some of the service people were Pack, some were Others. Of course on the night of the Great Hunt, there would be no Others present—only Pack. Tonight, however, was simply the meet and greet, and the Others working here thought we were members of an esoteric club. They didn't appear to be interested in the particulars. They weren't paid to be.

The bartender made us gin and tonics and the Councilor left him a two-euro coin before he led me toward the head table.

Several Councilors and their bond mates were already seated there, eating and talking among themselves.

Allerton didn't bring me to the head table, rather to one of the seven tables in front of it.

All ten seats were already occupied, but at a look from Allerton, one of the men got up with his plate and glass, and melted into the crowd.

Allerton gestured for me to take his place, gallantly pulling out my chair.

"Everyone, this is Constance Newcastle from Boston, Massachusetts," he introduced me. I noted he knew I'd moved. Maybe he'd read my name tag, because I couldn't fathom why he would have kept up with my life after pronouncing his judgment two years ago. "Constance, meet Liam Murphy. He's from Belfast."

An extremely attractive man with light brown hair and dark brown eyes lifted his gaze briefly from his contemplation of the contents of his wineglass and gave me a disinterested, polite smile. He was obviously bored. He smelled like he wanted to leave, but was constrained by good manners to stay at least through the first course.

Perhaps a kindred spirit? Someone else who was alone like me? I thought he might be interesting to talk to and was grateful to Allerton for giving me the opportunity to at least feel marginally like I belonged here. Maybe if I could draw him out into conversation he'd lose that bored scent and he might feel a part of things too.

"Hello," I said with a smile, as Allerton pushed in my chair then disappeared as if he'd never been there.

"Hi," said the man then took a sip of his wine and looked pointedly elsewhere.

The others at the table, having not been introduced, continued their own conversation and did not include me.

Cheeks flaming, I hid behind the water goblet at my place setting. How idiotic was I to think I could draw anybody out, or that anybody was interested in talking to me? How presumptuous I was to think that all the man needed not to be bored was to talk to me. Maybe he wasn't like me, maybe he very much fit in but didn't give a damn.

Liam Murphy's collar hid his pendant, so I couldn't tell if he was bonded, but he sat alone. I didn't think the man who'd vacated my chair had been with him. He'd probably been with the other eight people at the table who clearly knew each other. They all wore two or three-stone pendants. None of them seemed to wear name tags, and I became self-conscious of mine. These people were obviously from an influential pack—maybe nametags were beneath them?

Waiters came around with salads and took orders for the filet mignon, fish or chicken.

Liam Murphy ordered the steak, medium rare, and I did the same thing, hoping he didn't think I copied him.

The waiter asked me if I wanted red or white wine, and because Murphy had red, I chose white, which I instantly regretted, because I preferred red.

I drank my wine and tried to pretend I fit in with these people when I so obviously did not. All night long it had been one mortifying exchange after another. It was hard not to get discouraged, hard not to wish myself back in Boston. Why was it so hard to come back to life? Maybe that was the point. Maybe the things that mattered were hard sometimes and the measure of how much you wanted them was how much you were willing to endure to get them.

Or maybe I was just sitting at a table of rude and obnoxious people.

Liam Murphy had his body uncooperatively turned to the side. I thought he did it so he wouldn't catch my eye and have to talk to me. If my salad hadn't arrived just then, I would have returned to the table of feuding pack mates. At least they weren't rude, just enraged.

"So, Constance, is it true you used to be with the Riverglow pack in Hartford?"

I jerked my head up, surprised at being addressed.

One of the women across the table had finally deigned to speak to me, as if she knew what the hell she talked about. Her accent was British, so I didn't know how she could—surely news of the exile of one person from a tiny little pack in Connecticut hadn't traveled all the way across the ocean? That was all I needed.

My mind stuttered for a moment, because I didn't know what to say or do. *It's a simple question, Constance,* I lectured myself. *A one-word answer is all that's required. Maybe she's just making conversation. Breaking the ice.*

"Yes," I said cautiously.

"You're not the one who killed your bond mates in a stupid, careless car accident, are you?" She had long black hair and spiteful eyes. Her nails were like talons as she clutched her wineglass and smiled at me.

Next to me, Murphy shifted in his seat. Interested at last. But not in a good way.

Something stabbed at my heart. Humiliation? Guilt? Grief? A terrible sick combination?

"Because that's what I heard," the witch continued as if I weren't dying right in front of her. As if she didn't know she killed me with every word out of her mouth. "I talked to a man named Jonathan Archer and that's what he said. He ought to know, right? He is the Alpha in the Riverglow pack, isn't he?"

Jonathan. His name produced a dull glow of fury in my chest. I suddenly didn't feel as if I were dying anymore. I felt my jaw clench, so I deliberately relaxed and pretended a nonchalance I didn't feel. I'm sure I didn't fool anyone at that table. I must have reeked of defensive anger.

Liam Murphy stared at me now, his dark eyes narrow as he waited for my response. He leaned away from me as far as he could get without looking contorted. Body language is such a bitch.

"I don't really know." I shrugged. "He was Alpha, but I couldn't say if he is now. I haven't seen him in two years."

"Then you are that Constance," the witch crowed in delight. "How weird that Jason would put you at this table. We're not murderers here. Are we, Liam?" Her laughter was insulting.

The temperature at our table plummeted and I repressed a shudder.

Liam Murphy's eyes were pitch-black now. "Shut up, Mary," he suggested with a dangerous smile.

Then the bastard picked up his wineglass and left the table, stranding me.

No one spoke to me after that. It was like sitting in the middle of a void. As far as the rest of the table was concerned, I didn't exist. I certainly wished I didn't. I forced myself to eat my salad and choked down most of my steak, but said to hell with dessert and escaped to the bar.

The young bartender who had made my first gin and tonic hurried over to take my order and we talked for a while. He would break off to make drinks, but he'd always return to me. His name was Alain and he spoke rather good English, although I tried to practice my French on him and he was very kind about it.

Little by little I let go of my humiliation and relaxed. At least I wasn't at that damned table anymore. So what if I talked to an Other and not someone of the Pack? It was just what I needed—mindless conversation with somebody who did not know or care who I was.

As Alain mixed an impatient red-headed woman a complicated drink a young woman with her hair in a severe knot at the back of her head and a rather prim gown of cream and peach silk approached me.

She read my nametag carefully. "Constance, Councilor Allerton would like to see you privately. Please come this way." I figured she was an Advisor since she ran errands for a Councilor. She turned around and walked off, as though confident I would follow. I did. It's not as if I had a choice.

The prim girl led me out of the ballroom, up another twisting flight of stairs and into a long room with very high ceilings and narrow windows. One wall was stacked with bookcases. A ladder with wheels was propped against the shelves to reach the books near the ceiling.

Allerton sat on a curved chair of light brown silk, Liam Murphy on the matching sofa.

Because the room was long, it took forever to get to where they were seated. It felt as if I were on a catwalk in a fashion show. Both men watched me intently, and I became distinctly conscious of how low the neckline plunged on my decidedly red gown.

I took a seat on the sofa, hoping they viewed me more as a defiant red flame rather than an empty-headed high fashion model, I made sure to leave plenty of space between me and Liam Murphy. When I crossed my legs, I cursed under my breath as the slit in the side of my gown split to reveal almost my entire leg. Forget fashion model, now I was a damned femme fatale. Then and there I vowed never to listen to a French saleswoman in a dress shop ever again.

Allerton's eyes were frankly appreciative. Murphy looked up at my face and gave me a sarcastic smile, as if to congratulate me on a job well done.

As best I could I ignored him and accepted a snifter of brandy from Allerton as I settled back against the sofa. This time I deliberately let the slit fall where it may and received another obnoxious smirk from Liam Murphy.

He refused the brandy Allerton held out to him.

"Well, I suppose it's wise not to drink too much on an empty stomach. My people tell me you didn't eat your steak, Liam." Allerton crossed his legs in a masculine manner and fixed Murphy with a curious, displeased gaze.

"I wasn't aware you were all that interested in whether I ate my dinner or not, Councilor." A polite smile, just this side of condescending, crossed Murphy's face.

"I'm not. I had rather thought it was obvious I wanted you to talk to Constance."

Murphy added a sardonic raise of the eyebrows to his smile. The effect made me want to slap him and he wasn't even talking to me.

Allerton merely shrugged. He took a deliberate sip of his brandy.

"Liam, it's been close to three years since Sorcha died and you were a very good Alpha in your pack. Isn't it time you took up the reins of responsibility again and allowed yourself to live, perhaps?"

"You want me to go back to my former pack?" Muphy's eyebrows nearly disappeared into his hairline. "That's nice of you to be concerned. I planned to do that. Someday." His tone was just short of insolent as if he could not believe Allerton had made it his business to see his life rearranged.

"I suppose you'll rejoin your pack when you meet a new bond mate," suggested Allerton with an adroit smile. He glanced at me and I felt myself flush in shocked dismay as the implications became clear.

Liam Murphy looked no less horrified. His irritating smirk faded and his brows lowered as he thrust out his chin, jaw tight with belligerence.

"You're not serious? You want me to consider a woman who supposedly killed her bond mates through her own negligence?"

An icy chill suffused my face as the blood drained from my cheeks at the insult and, before I could stop myself, I snapped, "Your bond mate's dead too. How do I know you weren't negligent with her? It works both ways, you know."

There was murder in the glare Murphy directed at me, and something primal and feral leaped to life inside me. The two of us almost growled at each other, and if I'd been shifted, my hackles would have been raised to my ears. Bastard.

Allerton gave an apologetic cough, and said very gently, "Constance, Liam's wife was pregnant."

All my animosity vanished. What an idiot I was. A colossal, stupid idiot.

She must have died in childbirth. How awful for him.

"I'm sorry," I whispered, appalled at myself. "I'm so sorry."

Murphy's eyes remained flat and hostile. The apology was not accepted. His next words proved it.

"I realize with her history she might need a bit of assistance finding a new bond mate, but what's in it for you? What's your tie to her? Is she your mistress?"

I bit my lip and uncrossed my legs so they would be covered by fabric. If the damned door hadn't been fifty miles away, I would have slunk out. Instead, I tried to make myself as small as possible against the sofa cushions.

"Now you're insulting me as well as her," Allerton remarked, but there was steel in his voice.

Murphy caught himself up short, as if he realized he argued with a Councilor. But Alphas were very outspoken. They were used to being in charge. And Murphy was a definite Alpha. Even if he weren't currently in a pack, he was still Alpha material. He reeked of it.

"The two of you are here primarily to find new bond mates," Allerton said after a moment. The steel was gone from his voice, replaced with geniality. "All I'm suggesting is that you consider each other. That's all."

"Why?" Murphy asked.

"Why not?" Allerton jousted.

"He doesn't want to bond with me, Councilor. That's glaringly apparent. I would like to leave, please." I tried to stand, but Allerton forced me back down with just his gaze.

"But you would be interested in bonding with him?" His smile was full of encouragement. Murphy flashed me a sardonic grin while I sat there and wished I could melt into a bright red puddle. *Think before you speak, Constance*, I lectured myself.

The more time passed without me answering, the more Murphy regarded me as if I were some sort of disgusting bug he'd just realized crawled on the sofa next to him.

"Of course she would be. With her reputation, she'll need to take what she can get. I wasn't aware I had that same sort of reputation. And each minute further into this conversation I'm finding I care less and less. I'm here because my former pack practically begged me to come. I wasn't going to."

Allerton said, "I know."

He sighed and got to his feet. Murphy was on his like a shot and I was not far behind.

Ushering us to the door, he paused and looked at Murphy. "I wish you would at least consider Constance, Liam. Talk to her. You might be surprised at what you discover."

"I doubt it," said Murphy with another one of his damn grins. He was gone down the staircase and I went too, only slower so I wouldn't look as if I chased him. Plus I had to contend with stiletto heels and a tight dress. I prayed Allerton would not call me back and he didn't.

All the way down the stairs, I bounced back and forth between humiliation and rage.

Why had Allerton done something like this to me? What had I done to deserve such total mortification?

Techno music spilled out from the ballroom into the corridor. Beyond the arched doorway I saw dancers on the floor. It seemed as if everyone at the Gathering was dancing. Old, young, male and female, it didn't matter. They were all abandoned and flushed with pleasure as they moved to the beat. I wanted to dance too.

Grey, Elena and I used to dance in our home together and we'd go out to clubs.

The song was a familiar one—one I danced to a million times with them. If I closed my eyes I could even see their faces, sweaty and happy, as they danced with me.

Instead of joining the gyrating bodies, I went to my table and found my coat and purse.

The reception hall was nearly empty. A few people milled about. Six or seven couples sat on sofas as they talked or made out, but the former crush of people had migrated up to the ballroom.

On my way to the door, a couple entwined together pushed past me. There was all the room in the world to have gone around me, but they chose to go through me. The woman had a glass of red wine and she managed to spill it down the front of my gown.

With a dismayed gasp, I looked at her and recoiled. It was Nora from my old pack. With Jonathan. They both laughed and walked away without looking back.

As I tried to wipe the red wine off my gown with my fingers, I cursed. My new dress was ruined, of course. Perversely, now that it was, I mourned it even as I'd damned it in the room with Allerton and Murphy. It was the most beautiful and provocative dress I'd ever owned and now it was stained and worthless. Just like me.

"Club soda might help," said someone behind me. I whirled to see Liam Murphy, who stared at me with something almost like pity. I didn't think my humiliation could be any more soul-destroying, but I was wrong.

"I was leaving, anyway." I struggled to put on my coat. He helped me, although I didn't ask him.

"Aren't you supposed to be finding a new bond mate?" he wondered lightly as he adjusted the coat around my shoulders.

I searched for a clever comeback, but was too shaken to think quickly.

"Who were those two? You looked like you knew them." He spoke as if he had a right to know. Incredulous, I stared at him. First he couldn't escape me fast enough, and now he pretended to be interested in what happened to me?

"None of your business."

"It was rude."

It was my turn to smirk.

"Well, you ought to know." I waited a moment to see if he would evince any guilt. He stared at me, but when he didn't say anything, I turned around and walked out of the chateau, feeling his gaze burning into me as I left.

* * * *

The next morning it was a huge act of faith and courage for me to board the bus and go back to that damned chateau. How much humiliation should one person subject herself to? But I did it. By sheer will alone, I got on that bus. This time an elderly grandfather sat next to me. I offered him the window seat, but he said he preferred the aisle as the old bladder wasn't as reliable as it used to be then he cackled with laughter so I had to grin too. Suddenly, I didn't feel quite so much like I ran the gauntlet. Maybe I would even have a good time today.

Grandfathers and grandmothers were the salt of our subculture. They always added spice and knowledge and wisdom, plus they made you laugh at their bluntness.

We had to sign in again in the reception hall, which was tedious, but this time we were given shiny laminated name tags that pinned and were obviously meant to be kept through the rest of the Gathering.

There were lectures and workshops during the morning hours—*How to Succeed in Business Using Your Enhanced Senses, Areas to Hunt in Major Urban Locations, How to Cope With Your Wolf.* I'd heard them all before so I wandered around the chateau and marveled at the architecture and furnishings.

Lunch was a buffet in the ballroom. I sat at a table with a young mother and her bond mates. She spent most of the lunch on the phone to London, talking to the pack mate who had stayed behind to watch the children in the pack who were still too young to attend. Privately I thought the young mother ought to have stayed home with hers. She was obviously getting nothing out of the Gathering.

Her bond mates, one male and one female—an attractive blond with bold blue eyes—spent most of their time flirting across the table with each other, wordlessly, with their eyes. And, annoyingly, their feet. I had to pull mine under my chair to keep out of their way. It was very distracting and just about ruined my pleasure in lunch. That was a shame, because so far the day had sucked and the pasta in cream sauce could have been the highlight, but instead I bolted it down as I tried to avoid amorous feet and toes.

Naturally, no one talked to me. They all saw my pendant and after murmured hellos, ignored me. That was getting predictable.

Where was the lecture on surviving without a pack or a bond mate? I would go to that one like a shot.

After lunch there was a workshop on herbal remedies given by two old grandmothers, and I did attend that.

Plants and potions fascinated me. I loved crushing herbs with a mortar and pestle and distilling them with water and other liquids then mixing them into powders and measuring it into capsules. I loved reading about them and learning about their effects and their efficacy.

The repetition of the movement soothed me. It reminded me of days spent at my great-grandmother's side when I was a little girl.

The grandmothers, Hannah and Elise, praised those of us who grasped the concepts. They would test our knowledge, the grandmothers, by giving us only so many of the ingredients and asking us if we were making a remedy for stomach aches, for instance, what would we choose as the final ingredient.

I was right every time, but then I had read a lot of books and, growing up, I'd often stood at my own great-grandmother's knee to watch her concoct things.

That afternoon was the most peaceful of the Great Gathering.

We'd been told to bring our evening clothes with us and were provided with changing rooms, male and female. The room reserved for the females was sumptuously decorated with velvet-upholstered chaise lounges and French Impressionist paintings in elaborate frames. Antique mirrors placed in corners helped us determine whether we looked good. Porcelain bowls of potpourri were placed on marble-topped end tables. The scent of lavender and rose competed with expensive perfume.

Around six thirty, I changed into a short black dress with crisscross rhinestone straps and a pair of really cool silver stiletto sandals. The dress was cheap compared to the red gown, but I still thought I looked good as I twirled before one of the full-length mirrors.

Pack mates and bond mates chattered together and did each other's hair and makeup, but I, of course, did my own. I French braided my hair and tucked it up underneath, pinned in place against the back of my neck. My peridot pendant hung around my neck on a thicker, short silver chain, one I used for evening events.

I tried not to notice that nobody talked to me. However, it occurred to me that I wasn't talking to anybody either and communication is a two-way street after all.

A woman preened in the mirror next to mine, dressed in a long, white gown with bold black geometric designs. Her dark hair fell to the small of her back and glowed with purple highlights. She wasn't precisely beautiful, but she had an arresting, oval-shaped face, a large but distinctive nose and very red lips. Her eyes were brown and missed nothing.

She wore a pendant with two stones—one diamond, one garnet. It was the garnet that made me talk to her. Elena's birthstone had been a garnet. The woman's pendant had only two stones. Maybe there was a chance of a triad? If not, friendship? At the very least I would have a conversation.

Start with the little things, Constance, I told myself then gave her a friendly smile.

"Your dress is beautiful."

The look she gave me would have frozen fire.

She said something in a language that sounded maybe Russian or possibly Hungarian. I presumed she told me she didn't speak English. Or maybe to fuck off.

Someone nearby laughed, one of those cruel laughs that peeled away the armor of the soul and left you bare and bleeding.

My chin went up. I was alone, that was my only crime, and that was no crime—that was circumstance. Any of these bitches in their fancy dresses and immaculate makeup could find themselves alone at any moment. Their futures were not fixed. They had no real control over whether they would stay bonded or in love or anything. Why didn't they understand that?

Maybe I reminded them of that and they resented me for it. Maybe I exuded something, a scent of despair and futility.

If so, that, I could control.

I found the laughing woman and gave her my frostiest smile. "Was what she said really that funny?" I wondered and she gave me a deer-in-the-headlights stare. Her two companions looked as if they wanted to run away.

"She was rude actually," said the companion on the right, a short brunette with impossibly long eyelashes who was squeezed into a tight blue dress at least two sizes too small.

"I just told her that her dress was beautiful." I shrugged. "Oh, well, live and learn, I guess."

I turned to walk away, and the brunette said, "Your dress is better. I don't know if I like the design in hers. You're also much prettier than she is. By a long shot."

I smiled and turned back. "But I'll bet if we both walked into the room together, she'd get all the attention."

The brunette grinned. "Of course. Sex appeal relies very little on looks sometimes."

"It's attitude," I agreed, and she laughed. So did her companions.

"I'm Roxanne." The brunette introduced herself. "This is my bond mate Theresa, and our pack mate Lucy."

Lucy was the one who had laughed at me. Now she looked ashamed. "I don't speak much English," she admitted. Their accents were German.

"I'm Constance," I introduced myself.

"Your bond mate will be very proud to be with you tonight when he sees you in that dress," said Roxanne with an admiring look. I bit my lip.

"I don't have a bond mate," I confessed and waited for them to turn cold the way everyone had so far.

"Really? So you are here to find one, perhaps?" Roxanne gave me a jolly smile that demanded one in return. She wrapped a companionable arm around my waist and led me to one of the vacant vanity tables. "I like the way you did your eyes. Do mine that way, please?" She sat on the padded chair in front of the vanity and gazed expectantly at me. An array of designer makeup lay across the top of the vanity. Most of it still had the protective seal intact. One of the perks of attending the Great Gathering. I'd tucked a Dior lipstick and blusher into my purse earlier.

Lucy sat at the vanity table next to Roxanne's. Theresa brushed her long, dark hair while a curling iron heated. Both of them listened intently to my conversation with Roxanne. They seemed curious, not judgmental.

Roxanne closed her eyes as I swept some bronze eye shadow across her lids.

"Have you ever been bonded?" The question threw me a little, but I continued to trace the eye shadow along the bottom of her eyelid.

"Yes," I answered, but that was all I said.

"Theresa and I have been bonded with Helmut for eight years now. Or is it nine, Theresa?"

Theresa paused to think, the brush halfway through the thick fall of Lucy's dark hair.

"Nine," she decided as she resumed brushing.

"Helmut is a little bit of an idiot, but we love him." Roxanne's laughter was contagious and I joined in. I tried to picture what Helmut might look like. Tall and dark, I decided, with a perpetually perplexed expression on his face as he tried to keep up with his lightning dart of a bond mate.

"You will sit with us at dinner, of course," Roxanne declared when I finished doing her eyes. She studied her reflection with a smile of pleasure as she turned her head one way then another, and fluttered her lashes dramatically.

"Do I look American now?" She patted her hair and got to her feet. To me she looked distinctly foreign. Eye shadow could not change that.

She linked her arm with mine and led me out the door and down a short marble staircase. The ballroom doors were propped invitingly open and the four of us sailed through like queens.

Somewhere between eye shadow and the first glass of champagne, we became friends, and for the first time since I'd come to Paris, I felt as if I belonged to the Great Pack again.

We piled plates high with cheese and crackers and French delicacies then ate them with our fingers, laughing together.

Theresa secured a bottle of champagne from one of the cute waiters and we clinked glasses as we made toasts to each other and pledged friendship. We never stopped laughing.

Helmut turned out to be short and blond and not at all an idiot. He had a dry sense of humor that appealed to me, and I spent most of the cocktail hour trying not to choke because I laughed so hard.

"What is so funny?" A man enquired. He put a hand on Lucy's shoulder and smiled at us.

I looked up at him and my greeting died in my throat. "Rudi," I said at the same time he said, "Stanzie!"

It was my German boy from the Great Gathering when we were eighteen. Rudi Grunwald and I stared at each other, remembering the night we'd shifted for the first time together. Remembering how he'd stayed by my side when I'd yelped my way around the cane field terrified of the noise made by my own heart.

Rudi had not expected my strange, panicked reaction, but he'd stuck by me when all the others in our rag tag rebellious group of teens had fled.

My noise had attracted attention and the Alpha of my pack had shifted and come to our aid. We both had gotten into such trouble afterward we weren't allowed to see each other after that, but of course we did. We were eighteen. We'd wanted to bond together, but our packs told us we were too young. Technically, it had been true, but it could have been arranged if our parents hadn't been so stubborn. The fact we'd shifted together in defiance of our ways had not helped.

I remember we both cried when the Great Gathering was over and we had to go our separate ways—me back to Massachusetts, him all the way to Germany. We'd vowed to meet again and we had, but by then I'd bonded with Grey and I knew I'd let Rudi down. I could still remember the shocked disappointment on his face when I'd introduced Grey as my bond mate. Rudi had come from Germany to attend a Regional in New England—something I hadn't expected him to do since I hadn't heard from him after the Great Gathering. It had turned out Rudi had written me several letters, but I'd never received them. I'd suspected my father of intercepting them, but I'd never found out the truth.

Tonight I felt guilty at my cavalier treatment of him. He and Grey had not gotten along. He'd left the Regional early and I'd never thought to see him again, yet here he was across the table from me.

The German boy I'd once known had been replaced by a man. His once tall and gangly frame had filled out and I was sure under his suit coat his arms were toned and muscled, and he probably had a killer six-pack.

His face had matured and he was positively gorgeous. He looked so genuinely happy to see me. I remembered a sulky boy and here was a confident, happy man.

I jumped out of my chair as he came around the table and we embraced. I felt his heart beating as hard as mine as he cupped my face with his hands and stared down at me with delight.

"I'd hoped to see you, *schatzie*," he said, and there was real emotion in his voice. He really was glad to see me. There were no hard feelings, and it was good to see him. I didn't feel the crushing loss of Grey, I simply felt glad to see an old friend.

"Well, I'm here," I said. The lights above us dazzled my suddenly wet eyes.

"But where is..." He fumbled for a minute for the name but I wasn't fooled. He knew it. He just didn't want me to think he remembered it. "Grey?"

His eyes happened on my pendant and he bit his lip.

"Oh, *mein Gott*, have I said something bad?"

My smile faltered only a little bit.

"Grey's dead, Rudi," I explained. "In a car crash two years ago."

"Oh, Stanzie." He groaned and there were actual tears in his eyes as he hugged me, in an attempt to give me comfort. "I'm so sorry."

It had been easier to explain than I thought. Maybe because I got to say it first and it wasn't thrown at me as an accusation. I didn't want him to stop hugging me, but he did. He had to.

He sat next to me at the table and bent his head close to mine.

"You know Constance?" Roxanne was both surprised and pleased. Her face was somber, since I'd just revealed the death of my bond mate, but she clearly wanted to get back into the party and not dwell on death and other unhappy things. It seemed to me she had the right of things.

Rudi smiled and put his hand on top of mine.

"We met as teenagers at a Great Gathering a few years ago."

"We had our first hunt together. Hilariously disastrous because, of course, we had to sneak behind everyone's backs to do it," I explained, because I knew that would make Roxanne laugh and I was right. Everyone at the table joined in and the party atmosphere was restored.

We stayed together all that night, the five of us. We ate huge amounts of food, drank enormous amounts of alcohol, danced and flirted with each other, and had the best time together. The best time I'd had in years—two of them to be precise.

Grey and Elena retreated to a dark, unlit room in my mind. They were part of me, they always would be, but for the first time I allowed myself to envision a future that didn't include them and didn't feel as if I betrayed them or myself.

Lucy and Rudi turned out to be bond mates. I marveled at the odds of it as I looked between them and gauged their relationship. They loved each other, but I could tell they were not precisely in love, merely very comfortable. Had Rudi settled for her because he couldn't have me? It was a disconcerting thought.

Rudi and I danced together several times during the night. As it grew closer to the last dance, the songs slowed, became more seductive, less strenuous.

Rudi wrapped his arms around me and held me close while above us the crystal chandeliers glowed and gleamed like magic. It was all magic that night.

"I don't know why but I feel so right with you like this," he confided. "I always did, Stanzie. Why is it we didn't bond together?"

"We were too young," I replied as Madonna crooned *Crazy for You* in the background and other couples slowly revolved around us, satellites in the passion-drenched night.

"Not the second time," he remonstrated. "You were with Grey, but we could have still become a triad."

"Your English wasn't as good as it is now, Rudi. Grey could never understand what you said. I always had to explain things to him."

"I know." Rudi's face darkened at the memory and I longed to wipe away all of his frustration and resentment. That was years ago in a past that didn't exist anymore. It shouldn't have any power over him. "I went home from that Gathering and I threw myself in the study of English. I swore the next time I saw you I would be able to talk to him and maybe then he would consider me."

I decided not to bring up Elena. We'd both made lives for ourselves after we'd met, but he had always hoped one day I would be in his while I had never even imagined him in mine. I compared my happiness with Grey and Elena to his with Lucy and felt a stab of guilt that his had apparently fallen short.

"Was it so important to you, Rudi?"

"To bond with you? With you?" Rudi gazed at me, incredulous. "Don't you know, Stanzie, that I have adored you since that night we shifted for the first time?"

"How could you adore somebody who ran around the cane field yelping and screaming like a baby, trying to outrun her own heartbeat?" I giggled. I'd had a lot of champagne and the conversation was becoming way too serious for a night like this, for a song like this. I didn't want the sulky boy to come back. I wanted the confident, happy man.

"It was because you took the time for me. To try to understand me. The others brushed me off. I was the only German that year in our group. I couldn't get anyone to understand me but you. Only you, Stanzie. You helped me, I helped you."

Rudi brushed some hair from my face. My French braid was undoing itself. There had been a lot of very fast dancing and even more champagne. The room swirled and tilted in the most marvelous way. The way he looked at me, clutched at my heart. I was somewhere suspended between the past and present and, what was even better, the future.

He smiled at me then kissed me. It was one of those perfect kisses, perfect because the song, the room, the air and, most importantly, the other person was right.

We didn't stop dancing as we kissed and that added to the perfection. I felt him smiling against my mouth as his hands cupped my face and he tasted of champagne and something indefinable, something him, something I hadn't tasted in years, not since we'd said a tearful goodbye the last night of the Great Gathering when we'd both been eighteen.

"Tomorrow is the Great Hunt," he reminded me when the kiss ended. We were breathless and our hands traveled over each other's body, because we wanted more than just kisses. "Hunt with me, Stanzie?" His eyes were very blue as he looked down at me.

Transfixed, I nodded. I knew I should tell him about my wolf, but the champagne and music made me feel powerful, as if anything were possible. The hunt with him would be full circle. Our first hunt had been together. We'd become adults together. Now this one would herald something too. I had no doubts.

"I would very much like to bond with you, Stanzie. Please? It's rushed, I know, but not really because I've waited over ten years for this. It feels

Amy Lee Burgess

like forever to me. You will like Germany, I promise. And if you don't, we can go where you want. Wherever you want. What do you think? Will you even consider it?"

Consider it? It was everything I wanted. Everything I had come for. I hadn't even dreamed Rudi would ever figure in my future, but I could never tell him that. To me he'd been the past, but that could change.

It was fast. It was very fast. But I'd come to the Great Gathering to find a new bond mate. Last night I'd been alone and everyone had snubbed me, or looked right through me. Tonight I had made friends and been asked to become a bond mate. My head reeled at the strangeness of it all. Sometimes things went fast in our world because nobody liked to be without a pack.

"What about Lucy? We have to consider her too, Rudi," I pointed out. Even champagne could not make me forget everything.

"Lucy will be fine with this." Rudi was impatient because he wanted an answer.

"You ask her first. I can't answer you unless she agrees to this. You don't speak just for yourself, Rudi. She's your bond mate too."

"I would sever ties with her for you," he told me and he was serious.

I tried to feel flattered and not overwhelmed. I didn't want to think I was an obsession to him. He'd said he adored me, but he hadn't said he loved me. This was so fast and my head spun with so much champagne.

I wanted to lie down and sleep. When I woke life together with him would all make sense.

"I'm scaring you," he declared. He probably smelled my unease. His expression turned remorseful. "I'm sorry, Stanzie. Forgive me. Of course I'll ask her. You are right and wise. I'm too fast and too forward. It's just you always slip through my fingers. I don't want that to happen again."

"My old pack severed ties with me because they think I was reckless and careless and I killed Grey." I heard myself say it before I could stop the words.

His blue eyes went very wide.

"I was driving the car. We went over an embankment. Grey died in my arms, Rudi. I was driving the car and a Councilor from the Great Council had to come and decide whether I was innocent or guilty. Not the Regional. The Great Council."

Rudi digested this information silently for a moment.

"What did he decide? Not that I care," said Rudi, but it was clear from his expression a part of him did.

"I was absolved of blame." I swallowed an obstruction in my throat and most of the magic of the night disappeared. I wanted to disappear.

Rudi tilted my chin up so I was forced to look at him.

"Fuck your former pack," he said, his words slow and distinct. His eyes blazed. "I don't care, Constance. Nothing you've done has changed my feelings for you. The Great Council cleared you. Accidents happen."

I wondered if he thought this particular accident had been opportune for him and I mentally slapped myself. That wasn't fair. That wasn't right. And if I allowed myself to go there, I might never find my way back to feeling good about him ever again. And he was good. Rudi was a good man.

"Oh, Rudi," I said, unsure of everything and he hugged me, more like a friend than a lover, and that helped so much. I was drunk and stupid.

We sat together on the bus back to Paris, huddled in each other's arms. It was cold at first, even with the heat blowing full blast, but when it did become warm we still held each other.

Roxanne and Theresa sat slumped together, asleep, in the seat behind us. Lucy was across the aisle, also asleep. She'd put her hand on my shoulder as we'd boarded the bus, and that gesture let me know she had no objections to me. She had told me without words that she would not stand in the way and she welcomed me.

"Yes," I murmured dreamily as the bus chuffed to stop in front of my hotel. Rudi and the others stayed at a different hotel, another stop or two away from mine.

"Yes, what, Stanzie?" Rudi roused himself from a semi-doze and brushed more hair from my face as the bus doors creaked open.

"I will bond with you and Lucy," I told him and his whole face lit up adorably.

"I will make you so happy," he vowed and I believed him. I really did.

He kissed me goodbye, and I nearly didn't make it off the bus before the driver pulled back into the sluggish, early morning traffic.

I stood on the cold sidewalk and watched Rudi wave goodbye through the bus window and wished I'd gone with him to his hotel. There was no reason for me to sleep alone at mine. I could have taken the Metro back in the morning to get dressed.

As I thought to myself that this would be the last night I would ever sleep alone, I smiled.

Chapter 3

The Great Hunt commenced at sunset. The ballroom had been transformed into what could be described as an orgy room—pillows on the floor for some, mattresses swathed in bold-colored sheets and screens set up for those who preferred privacy, but there was plenty of room for those who wanted to be seen and joined.

There was music but no alcohol. Instead, grandmothers and grandfathers passed out bottled water. Half the bottles had blue labels, half of them pink. It was an affectation, a frivolity. A lively old grandmother handed me two bottles when I walked in alone.

"Pink for you, blue for him, dearie!" She gave me a lascivious wink.

We avoided alcohol before we shifted. Alcohol dehydrated, and if we drank too much before shifting, the day after was an agony of muscle cramps and soreness. Instead we drank water. Lots of it. Instead of muscle cramps the next day, we pissed a lot. I'd experienced the muscle cramps and I much preferred staying close to a bathroom.

The bottles were ice cold and dripped with condensation. I held them away from my body as I looked around for Rudi. He'd given a presentation the last half of the afternoon, something to do with his job. He had tried to explain his work to me on the bus ride back to the chateau that morning, but I was lost in the technicality of it. He was an inventor. He'd made his pack rich with a patented device he'd come up with that aided telecommunications. He'd gotten that far before my eyes apparently glazed over and he'd laughed and changed the subject to spare me.

The presentation was technical and deadly dull, he informed me when I told him I would attend. "Don't be silly, Stanzie, we'll see each other at the Great Hunt."

So I'd spent the latter half of the afternoon with Roxanne, Theresa and Lucy, wandering around the chateau and talking. Roxanne and Theresa planned to participate in the Great Hunt. Lucy decided to sit it out. Because of me, of course, but she confided she didn't much like group hunts and she'd see us afterward at the late-night supper.

I liked her more, which was a good thing considering we would be bond mates soon.

Two nights from tonight, the bonding ceremony would take place. My head was full of the idea that I was going to move to Berlin and join a pack and be a part of things again. I would have time to truly fall in love with Rudi, something I felt as if I were already doing. He reawakened so many things inside me. It was a jumble of desire, longing and anticipation and, yes, fear. Fear of the unknown. Anything could happen. I was not the same Constance who had boldly bonded with Grey, then Elena, secure in the knowledge I was loved and would be with someone until I was old and either they died first or I did. It would be so far in the future as to be almost unimaginable.

Rudi had secured one of the mattresses behind a painted screen of a Paris street, which featured a brasserie and wrought-iron tables and chairs, the hint of a waiter lurking behind a door.

He was sprawled on the mattress as he drank from a bottle of water. It had a blue label. A pink-labeled bottle rested beside him.

I tossed him my blue-labeled bottle and he tossed me the pink one.

"Properly hydrated." I sank beside him, smiling. I felt a little shy, a little turned-on. This would be so much easier, this group thing, with alcohol, but it dehydrated. Plus it disoriented. Everyone wanted to be sharp in wolf form. What was the point of blunted senses? All afternoon I'd both looked forward to and dreaded this moment. I wanted so much to participate, but I was also scared. Today no champagne clouded my judgment and I knew I should tell Rudi about my wolf and what to expect, but I found myself tongue-tied with lust. It drove all sense of responsibility and trepidation out of my head.

Later, I told myself. *You can tell him later, Stanzie.*

Rudi had on a pair of dark jeans and a blue sweater. It had rolled up a bit to reveal a slice of his taut stomach. I reached out and ran my hand up under the fabric to his chest. Yes, he was muscled in all the right places.

I hadn't had sex in so long. No one had touched me, or had been there to touch back. I craved it like a drug that drove all sense from my mind.

Your wolf needs to be discussed, Stanzie, I lectured myself, but in the next breath the thought was gone and all I wanted was the connection with another person from the Pack. And him. I wanted him.

He grinned as I touched him and tossed his empty water bottle to the floor. Something flashed across his face, a grimace.

"Your hand's cold," he told me. Of course it was. I had an ice-cold bottle of water. He unscrewed the cap of the bottle I'd given him and drank some. I finished my first bottle, and as I reached for the second, he playfully grabbed me and pushed me down onto the mattress so he could kiss me.

"Why are you so serious?" he wondered between kisses. At first they were light, but gradually they deepened. He slid his hands beneath my sweater and I didn't mind that they were cold. Besides, he only teased me. Before I knew it, he sat up, back propped against the wall.

"Drink more water," he suggested with a slanted grin. He touched his bottle to mine.

An amorous couple passed by then. They almost had to walk across us to get to the screened mattress near ours.

I looked up at the interruption and found myself staring into the face of Liam Murphy. He was being tugged along by a gorgeous brunette with sultry brown eyes.

He gave me one of his damned grins, and I almost threw my water bottle at his face, but that would have been a waste of good hydration.

Instead I ignored him. The brunette said something that made him laugh and they were gone, thankfully.

I turned back to Rudi. I was going to say something disparaging about Murphy, but I didn't because Rudi was very pale. He was sweating too.

"I don't feel very well, Stanzie." His blue eyes slitted against some internal pain.

"Maybe you should drink some water," I suggested, not knowing what the hell to do. And he did. "I'll go find a grandmother. Do I think I should?"

A grandmother would know what to do. Maybe he'd eaten something bad at lunch. I felt a momentary relief that I probably wouldn't be participating in the Great Hunt and was immediately ashamed of myself. Coward.

Remorsefully, I reached out to touch his face and he grabbed my wrist with his hands hard enough I thought I might scream, only I was too shocked.

"Stanzie," he gasped, his eyes locked pleadingly to mine. Then he died.

The light left his eyes. Something bright and essential leaped from his still body and dissipated into the nothing.

His body convulsed, his fingers slackened and his arms fell to his sides. His eyes—his empty eyes—stayed open. But he saw nothing.

"Rudi?" I choked out. My disbelieving hand reached out to touch his face and my fingers communicated the truth to my stuttering brain.

I screamed then. I screamed and couldn't stop because this was not happening. This was not real. It was a nightmare and if I screamed loud enough I would open my eyes and be in my little single bed in the Paris hotel. The day would just be starting, it would not be ending. Not this way.

The screen collapsed when I blundered into it, as I shrieked both his name and my wordless horror.

Somebody grabbed me, forced me down to the ground and I struggled, kicking and clawing, but he was stronger.

"Stop. Constance, stop screaming. Stop screaming right now!" There was an Irish lilt in the man's voice, more Irish than he'd sounded the night before when I'd met him. He was scared too but in way more control than I was.

"You've got to stop screaming and tell me what happened!" Liam Murphy had lipstick on his cheek. His white shirt was half unbuttoned. His hair was tousled as if someone had passionately run her fingers through it. He hadn't shaved and my scrabbling fingers rasped against the stubble on his cheeks and chin.

"He's dead! Rudi is dead!" I screamed at him. I hit out at him, tried to hurt him because Rudi was dead and there was nothing I could do about it.

I couldn't take a deep breath and my head felt as if it were full of helium as it tried to float away from my body. My eyes wouldn't focus. Murphy's face alternated between huge and miniscule as I struggled to drag enough air into my lungs to keep from suffocating. My skin was clammy with cold perspiration one moment and then dry and burning hot the next.

Murphy held me down, his face tight with determination. Even though I couldn't see straight, his gaze never left mine, not for a second, even when a pandemonium of noise and movement erupted behind us where Rudi's body rested.

"Jesus Christ," somebody said. "Jesus Christ."

"Was it poison? In the bottle? Look, there's an empty bottle near him and another one half full. Was something in it?"

Babbling voices competed with each other as Liam Murphy and I stared at each other.

I'd stopped screaming, but my heart pounded so fast and hard I thought I was dying. Things got very bright then very dim and the voices got louder then softer. Sometimes I couldn't understand them, sometimes I could.

"Rudi's dead," I said again. Conversationally. Trying it out so it would take on some sort of meaning.

Murphy sat on top me, legs to either side of my torso, pinning me down. He had both arms up above my head, wrists together, blocking me from any movement.

His chest heaved from exertion or maybe stress. His gaze never, ever left mine.

"I'm going to let you up now," he said, also conversationally. "And you're not going to run or scream. Are you?" The Irish lilt was more subdued now. I realized he was conscious of it and guarded against how much of it he revealed in everyday, ordinary speech.

I shook my head, because my heart beat too hard for me to speak.

"You need to answer me, Constance. I'll not let you up until I know you can do what I ask you to do. So I'm asking again. You're not going to run or scream, are you now? You're going to stand by me and do whatever they tell you to do. They're going to want to ask questions and you're going to answer them and you're not going to scream and get hysterical. Tell me I'm right."

"You'll stay with me?" I begged. I felt that maybe—maybe—I could do it if at least one familiar face was in the background somewhere. "I'm so alone, Murphy. I don't have anyone and I'm scared."

"Don't be scared," he said. "I'll stay with you if you promise not to run or scream. Deal?"

People were gathered around us. I felt them watching us. Some were fascinated, some impatient—all of them were confused. There was anger too. I could smell that.

"Deal," I said and he nodded in solemn approval of my decision. He helped me to my feet, glaring at the ones who tried to step forward.

"My mouth is so dry," I whispered because it was. It hurt it was so dry.

"Give her some water," Murphy snapped.

"No, not that one. We need to analyze that," a woman protested.

"Just get her some goddamned water, someone, please!" Murphy was angry now. On my behalf? Or at everything, including me?

Someone handed me a half-drunk bottle of water and I gulped at it gratefully, as I clutched it in my hands while Murphy guided me by the elbow out of the ballroom. He knew where we were going. I didn't. All I knew was that Rudi was dead and the water tasted divine.

* * * *

"What did you put in the water, Constance?" It was the same question over and over again. It had been hours now since they'd brought me to the little room with the white marble fireplace and the museum-quality furniture. The grandfather clock in the corner had chimed every quarter hour and I'd heard the distinctive sound thirteen times now. I was numb and could no longer felt the empty water bottle I had crushed between my hands.

Murphy sat beside me. His temper had spiraled up and up with each chime of that damned clock. At some point he'd re-buttoned his shirt, but he still had the lipstick smudge—now faded—across one cheek. His hair was still a tousled mess, his dark eyes flat and murderous.

A French woman from the Great Council, Celine Ducharme, asked most of the questions. Jason Allerton was there too, but mostly he was quiet. Listening. Taking notes. Not on paper but inside his head. Three Advisors were present. They were the ones who took notes on paper—

one in French, one in English, one in German. The German one was for Rudi's pack.

Rudi's pack snarled and paced on the other side of the door. I heard them sometimes. Lucy sobbing, Roxanne trying not to, Theresa talking in fast German with a pack member I had not met and did not want to meet, considering the circumstances.

The first time Celine Ducharme asked me that question I had stared at her blankly, because things weren't making much sense.

"She's in shock, goddamn all of you," Murphy had snarled. "Why can't this wait? Let her get herself together. Can't you see she's barely even hearing you?"

While Ducharme's eyes had narrowed menacingly when Murphy swore at her, Allerton had simply sat in his chair, silent, and calm. He had a very Zen quality to him I envied, even though at that point I felt more out of my body than in it.

Councilor Ducharme had glared daggers at Murphy then repeated her question to me, leaning in toward my face, glowering. Her lipstick was a shade between coral and scarlet. There were fine lines in the skin around her mouth. She balanced between middle and old age. I figured she had ten years max left on the Council before she became a grandmother. There were no grandmothers on the Councils. Or grandfathers, for that matter. No, one morning soon enough she would not be able to cover the wrinkles with skillful makeup and all the hair dye in the world wouldn't cover the gray. If she hadn't gracefully stepped down from the Great Council, she would be asked to leave it to exist on the charity of her pack. That day, it seemed to me, couldn't come soon enough.

Murphy's voice had dripped sarcasm. "What kind of a kangaroo court is this? You've already decided she's guilty, haven't you?"

"What did you put in the water, Constance?" Celine Ducharme asked it again for maybe the twentieth time.

"Nothing," I answered for maybe the twelfth time. I was gradually regaining my sense of surroundings. I had to pee—all that goddamned water.

"I grow tired of this." She gave the room a sour look and Murphy gave her one of his trademark smirks, for once not aimed at me.

"I was tired of this three and half hours ago," he said.

"You can leave any time you like, *monsieur*!" Ducharme flared. "I'm not even sure why you're here? Why are you here? You saw nothing. You explained that much already."

"She's only said she didn't put anything in the water about fifteen times now. You're still asking the same question, though. Why don't you ask me what I saw over and over again? Maybe I'll change my answer the way you want her to change hers."

"I believed you," declared Ducharme. Ice frosted her words so that I shivered involuntarily.

"I'm not getting anything off her that indicates she's lying, Councilor," argued Murphy.

"The Pack are not as easy to read as Others are, *monsieur*," the Councilor reminded him. "She could be very good at this. I think she must be. After all he died right in front of her and here she is being defiant and refusing to cooperate. Highly suspicious."

"She is cooperating. Just because she's not telling you what you want to hear doesn't mean she's not cooperating." Murphy's jaw was tight and he had to almost force the words out.

Ducharme gave him a pitying smile.

"You have nothing that ties her to this man's death tonight," Murphy's mouth twisted in disgust.

"When the tox screens come back from the water analysis, we'll see about that, *Monsieur* Murphy."

Murphy glanced irritably at his watch and shook his wrist as if he could make time go faster that way. "You aren't going to keep us boxed up in here until then, are you?"

"As I've said repeatedly, you can leave whenever you like. In fact, I wish you would. Gerald, show this man to the door please."

Allerton lifted his hand, but it was enough to cause the young Advisor, Gerald, to sit back down looking rather relieved. I would have been relieved too. By the expression on Murphy's face, it would have been hell trying to kick his ass out the door.

"Elise Benoit tells me you are very good with herbs, Constance." Celine Ducharme leaned forward in her antique chair, her brown eyes alight with suspicion. Her thin face looked sucked in, as if she perpetually tasted a fresh slice of lemon under her tongue. "You were the star pupil in the herbal lecture yesterday, weren't you?"

I looked at the crushed plastic water bottle in my hands and wished I could go to the bathroom. In about ten minutes, I would have a very embarrassing accident.

"I like to crush up the herbs and ingredients and measure them into capsules and liquids. It's soothing. It clears my mind," I said.

"Aha," declared Celine Ducharme, as if I had confessed to something unspeakable.

"What did you make yesterday in the herbal lecture?" Murphy asked me. When he talked to me, his voice was almost gentle, the sarcasm gone, but his jaw was still exquisitely tight.

I had to think about it, because mostly all I could concentrate on was not peeing myself.

"We made a remedy for stomach aches and one for headaches." I was rather proud of myself for being able to recall that under the circumstances.

"No poisons? You didn't make any poisons?" Now Murphy sounded sarcastic, but he talked mostly to Councilor Ducharme.

"No poisons." I shrugged.

"You'd better lock her up, Councilor. She's guilty of making a home remedy for stomach aches and headaches. Pure evil. We can't let that sort of knowledge roam free."

"Be quiet," snapped Celine Ducharme. "If one is good at one part of herbalism, why wouldn't one be good at another? Like poison?"

"Is that what the grandmothers are teaching nowadays? How to poison people? Not my grandmother. Not any grandmother that I ever knew."

"They know poisons. They have to know certain ones. Taken in small doses they cause things to happen that may be necessary sometimes." The Councilor's words were vague but we all got the meaning.

"Constance, did you try to give Rudi a home abortion this afternoon? Was he pregnant and not Alpha in his pack?" Murphy enquired, straight faced. One of the Advisors, the English one—Gerald—let out a snort of laughter and quickly apologized under the searing glare of Celine Ducharme.

"If I don't get to the bathroom in about two seconds, I'm going to piss myself," I said, because I didn't care anymore and it was the truth.

This time the French Advisor was the one to laugh. Even Murphy's tight jaw unclenched a little to allow a tiny smile.

"Angelique, escort her." Councilor Ducharme rolled her eyes in exasperation. "Don't let her try anything."

"I'm not going to escape out the bathroom window if that's what you're afraid of. I won't even try to give myself a home abortion in the hopes of killing myself by accident. I just have to pee." I rose to my feet with alacrity and hoped the damn bathroom wasn't a football field away.

I exited to the sound of smothered laughter.

I don't think anything in my life even came close to feeling as good as taking that particular piss did. Not sex, not a massage, not a run in the forest. Nothing.

The Advisor, Angelique Roget, waited by the door for me. She was petite and pretty, very French, with long, blond hair she'd pulled back into a silver barrette. She had her notebook in hand and pretended to study it as I came out into the hall, marveling at the relief.

"Did you love him?" She looked up from her notebook. We stared at each other. The wind outside blew around the eaves of the chateau and a tree limb scraped at a window across from us. The shadow of it crossed us momentarily, rendering us faceless.

When I could see her eyes again, I said, "We were going to be bond mates. We were going to bond at the ceremony later this week." I confessed it as if it were a crime.

"Why would you kill him?" She flipped her notebook shut. "Sometimes I detest my job."

Celine Ducharme was, to put it bluntly, pissed off when we returned. Murphy smirked and Allerton just sat there with legs crossed at the ankle, hands steepled in front of his face, concealing his expression.

The tox screen results had arrived. They were inconclusive.

"Inconclusive does not mean he was not poisoned!" Councilor Ducharme spat, her straw-like hair whipping around her face as she stalked around the fireplace. Flames crackled in the grate and I smelled the scent of burning birch wood. It was such a light green smell. Like spring.

"What the hell does that mean? They didn't find anything, Councilor, because there was nothing to find." Murphy stopped smirking, and clenched his fists, his eyes dangerously dark.

"It just means they didn't look for the right things!"

"What?" Murphy's jaw dropped. "The grandmothers didn't know what the hell to look for? Bullshit. I'm calling bullshit."

"You better stop swearing at me, *monsieur*! I don't know who you think you are, but I grow very tired of your constant interference in this interrogation!" Celine Ducharme stabbed a stick-thin scarlet-tipped finger at him and, if she could have, she would have ripped his eyeballs out with her fingernails.

"This whole interrogation is a farce. This woman was going to have sex with Rudi Grunwald, she wasn't plotting murder! I have no idea why you insist on believing this wasn't some sort of tragic accident. Maybe he had some medical condition we don't know about, or maybe an allergic reaction to something!"

"Why wouldn't that show on the tests if it were an allergic reaction? Something would be in his bloodstream!"

"A medical condition then. A heart attack."

"He was thirty-two years old. You are delirious, *monsieur*!"

"There's going to be an autopsy, right? Not just a goddamned inconclusive tox screen I hope!"

"Of course there will be an autopsy. It's already going on!" Celine Ducharme snarled.

I saw it in my treacherous mind then. Rudi lying dead and pale on a table, knives slicing into his body so measurements and samples could be taken before he was sewed back up when they were through. And he'd never laugh anymore, or shift into a big silver-gray wolf and run through the forest with his pack mates ever again.

Something must have showed on my face, because they all looked at me then and the room fell silent.

"She was going to bond with him," Angelique declared with a suddenness that startled all of us. "Councilor Ducharme, Constance was going to bond with him at the ceremony on Friday. Why should she murder him? She had nothing to gain and everything to lose."

Allerton's eyes crinkled as he smiled behind his fingers. I had to wonder how long Angelique would keep her job. Maybe she didn't care. She detested it, anyway. Sometimes.

Murphy stared at me. I guess he hadn't known Rudi and I were going to bond.

"Is that what she told you?" Celine Ducharme stalked to the door, ripped it open and a moment later Lucy stood on the carpet in front of us, her eyes red rimmed, her nails bitten short.

"Yes, it's true," she confirmed when the question was put to her. "Rudi told me last night on the bus after we dropped Stanzie off at her hotel. She was going to bond with us. He was so happy. We all were." Her voice dropped and she looked at me. I could tell she wanted to ask me if I'd killed her bond mate. I shook my head no, even though she didn't ask and her breathing seemed to come a little easier. She gave me a small, very sad smile. She believed me.

"He was not Alpha in your pack. Did he clear this with *Monsieur* Bergen? Your Alpha?" Celine wouldn't let it go. She was incensed for some reason at the thought I might have bonded with Rudi.

"Rudi was acting Alpha here at the Great Gathering, because Willem stayed home with Greta and their newborn twins. Rudi was free to take another bond mate. We want more triads in our pack, anyway, Councilor. It would not have been an issue."

"Not even if Willem knew her history? Knew that she'd killed her own former bond mates? He wants that sort of filth in his pack, Lucy?"

Lucy gasped. So did most of the room. I didn't. I just looked down. I wondered what had happened to my plastic water bottle. Now my hands didn't have anything to do.

"Excuse me, Councilor, but Constance was cleared of all culpability in that regrettable accident. In fact, if you might recall, I am the one who actually investigated the event, and if anyone in this room can state her guilt or innocence in the matter, it would be me, wouldn't you say?" Allerton lowered his hands to reveal his face. His expression was impatient and angry. "We've all had accidents in our lives. Does that make us all filth? Are you so blameless?"

Ducharme bristled. She almost growled and, except for the fact she was such a bitch and I could not imagine any man voluntarily getting near her for sex, I would have bet she wanted to shift and rip Allerton's throat out.

"She was driving the car, Jason."

"The car was examined after the accident, Celine. There was nothing wrong with it."

"By someone of the Pack?" Ducharme demanded.

"Yes, by one of the grandfathers of the Riverglow pack, in fact. Who knew and loved all three of them."

I saw Grandfather Tobias in my mind then. I remembered driving the Mustang to his little house in Manchester so he could see it. When Grey gave me the car for my birthday, he had asked me where I wanted to drive first and it was to Grandfather Tobias. He knew cars. He was a mechanic.

"That doesn't prove anything. Maybe she didn't tamper with the car, maybe she drove off the embankment on purpose."

"Oh, for fuck's sake," raged Murphy. "What for? And remember, she was in the car too. Unless you're saying it was a murder suicide pact, why the hell would she do something like that? You're grasping at straws!"

"I don't like the way this woman is always involved in tragedy!" Celine Ducharme narrowed her already small brown eyes and glared at us all. "Once perhaps. Twice strains the credulity, and I, for one, do not want to wait for the third time to prove me right."

"Why do you hate her? What has she done to you? Did you have a thing with Rudi Grunwald maybe?"

The sound of Ducharme's palm slapping Murphy's face was loud and shocking, but he only smirked.

"You have lipstick on your cheek," she spat at him. I inwardly smiled to myself, because I thought she was incensed she did not get a rise. "All night you've had lipstick on your cheek."

"You don't say?" He continued to smirk and walked to an ornate gilt mirror hung by the door. He peered into it and regarded both the bright red palm print on one cheek and the lipstick smear on the other. "I'm really getting to the ladies today. Must be the Irish in me."

Angelique giggled.

The English Advisor's stomach growled and he looked horrified.

"We're all starving, it's not just you," Murphy commiserated. He looked at the grandfather clock in the corner and it obligingly struck ten o'clock.

If Rudi hadn't died, the Great Hunt would be in full swing now. As it was, everyone had gone back to Paris if they had hotels, or retreated to their rooms in the chateau if they didn't.

"This isn't over. We shall reconvene tomorrow when we have the autopsy results," Councilor Ducharme decided, her mouth curved in a petulant scowl.

Chapter 4

I wasn't allowed to go back to Paris. I was assigned a tiny room that was obviously meant for a servant. I could barely turn around in it, and I think that was the point.

I wasn't locked in but only because the bathroom was down the hall. There was nowhere to run. Not to mention I didn't have any reason to run, because I hadn't done anything.

They gave me a tray of food but I couldn't eat it. I kept thinking of Rudi and how except for the fact he was dead and being dissected somewhere below in the chateau, we would be shifted into wolves at that moment and running together and wrestling, maybe noses to the ground in pursuit of some small prey. My stomach churned.

I put the tray on the floor in the hall by my door and went to the tiny bed. It was stuffed under the eaves of a slanted ceiling, one side shoved into the wall, and I had to be careful when I lay down, or I would have given myself a concussion. I only hoped I didn't have a nightmare and jerked upright in the middle of the night, or I was going to have one hell of a serious headache.

Opposite the bed was a window, and I left the blind and curtains open so I could see the moonlight. A tall tree cast a ghostly shadow and the leaves rustled in the November wind. It was a lonely sound. A cold sound.

I didn't know if I could fall asleep, if my mind would give me such mercy, but I did finally. If I dreamed, I don't remember.

* * * *

A breakfast buffet was set up in the grand ballroom complete with crepes and omelet stations. I thought about the crepes, but in the end I took a cup of coffee and a croissant and sat at a table near the windows so

I could look out at the fountains. To say I was in a bad mood was putting it mildly.

It was a gorgeous day—sunny and bright. It seemed an affront to Rudi's memory. It should at the very least have been overcast.

Instead I squinted against the painful glare of the sun on the water and tried to drink my coffee black, because there was no cream on the table and I didn't feel like walking around trying to find some. There was sugar. Thank the gods for the small things at least.

A shadow mercifully blocked the exuberant sunshine and I watched Liam Murphy pull out the chair opposite me. He had a plate piled high with what appeared to be a dozen scrambled eggs plus country ham, maybe a whole pig's worth, and toast. Six slices.

"Didn't eat dinner last night." He shrugged as I eyed his plate. He offered it to me when he noticed my croissant. I had crumbled pieces of it onto the china plate, but one bite had been all I could stomach. Maybe if there'd been some goddamn cream for the coffee I could have choked down more.

He had cream in his coffee. A whole boatload of it and I felt real resentment burn my throat like acid.

As I glared at him, he pushed half the eggs, a third of the country ham and two slices of toast onto my plate. My croissant was buried under the avalanche.

The food smelled surprisingly good, which made me twice as resentful.

"Eat." He waved his fork at my plate.

He looked up and gestured to a white-coated waiter who swerved across the room to stand at our table.

"Can we have some orange juice and cream?" Murphy asked in perfect French, which galled me, because it was much better than mine. I was beginning to hate this man, even though he'd stuck up for me. Maybe that was precisely why I was beginning to hate him because now I owed him.

"I don't want orange juice," I said just to be spiteful. I spoke in French to prove he wasn't the only person at this table who could speak the language.

The waiter brought it, anyway. I refused to believe it was my accent. It was Murphy. Alpha male bastard fuck.

I did, however, fall upon the cream and poured at least half the pitcher into my coffee. It was lukewarm by that point and the cream didn't help that, but it tasted better and I drank it in two swallows.

Murphy fell to consuming the food on his plate. I mostly moved mine around with my fork, but I did eat one whole slice of toast and part of a piece of the country ham. I also drank the orange juice before I remembered I said I hadn't wanted it.

Aside from a brief grin, Murphy didn't say anything, which was good for him, because there was enough juice left in my glass to throw in his face.

"Ready to run the gauntlet this morning?" He set his fork down on his plate, looking almost surprised to see how empty it was. He pulled his coffee cup toward him. The spoon rattled on the saucer and a little bit of coffee sloshed over the rim. It was the color of those caramel crèmes that came in plastic-wrapped cubes when I was a little girl. I used to use them to pull out my loose teeth. Anything just a little bit wiggly came right out when stuck to one of those suckers. I could almost taste the sugar-coated blood in my mouth just looking at his cup.

"I'm hoping I can just sit here all day and they've forgotten about me," I muttered as I debated whether I wanted another piece of toast. I did want more coffee. Murphy saw me looking at my cup and did that thing with his hand again so the waiter appeared like magic. I could never get them to respond to me that quickly.

"More coffee please. And orange juice." He winked at me and I ignored him.

"They aren't going to forget about you, Constance."

"No shit."

"Well, has a night's rest done you any good? Are you actually going to defend yourself today, or you are going to rely on me like you did yesterday?" He took a swallow of his coffee and I wanted to reach out and knock it out of his hand so it splashed all over his cashmere sweater. Why the hell was he wearing a cashmere sweater, anyway? It was a crewneck. Dark brown. I had always had a thing for crewneck sweaters. They were sexy, especially if the man didn't wear another shirt underneath it just like Murphy wore it and...

I made myself look at the fountains, and the searing sunlight nearly blinded me, which drove all thoughts of considering Murphy as anything approaching sexy right the hell out of my head—which was exactly what I wanted.

The mind was a strange and stupid place sometimes. Here I was in big, huge trouble and I all I could think about was how sexy crewneck sweaters were. Defense mechanism my ass. I was a goddamned idiot.

"You don't have to defend me today. You didn't have to defend me yesterday, either." I huffed then had to shut up because the waiter returned with orange juice and a carafe of hot coffee.

I drummed my fingers in an impatient rhythm on the white table top until the waiter was gone before I snapped, "I don't even know why you're sitting here."

"Maybe I felt sorry for you." He shrugged with a malicious gleam to his dark eyes.

"Oh, fuck you, I don't need..." Real anger burned hot in my gut, even if it were misplaced and directed against the wrong person, and he just sat there with that grin, pleased to have provoked me. That's when the Advisor, Angelique, came up to our table.

I clamped my lips shut around the words I had been about to scream. My face was flushed and my pulse rate rocketed off the charts.

"They'll be ready for you in five minutes," she announced as if the top of my head were not about to split open so hot lava could spew all over the place.

She walked away, her hips swaying in a tight gray skirt with a chic Parisian ruffled hem. I caught Murphy looking at her ass and he saw me catch him. He winked and I tried really hard not to think about how much I wanted to kill him.

"You don't have to come," I said instead. I knew I was being ungracious and belligerent, considering he'd stuck up for me the night before. But I hadn't asked him to and I had no idea what crazy reasons he had for doing what he'd done. They couldn't have all been because he was a nice guy and doing me a good turn. Balls to that.

"Are you kidding? I wouldn't miss this show for anything, Constance. Besides, I'm waiting with bated breath to find out what Allerton really wants. You wait, he'll tip his hand today. I've come this far, I want to see how it ends."

"Allerton?" I blinked at him, pretending I didn't know what he meant, but he just grinned. He got to his feet, because it would take us the rest of the five minutes to find the goddamn room again. I thought I knew where it was in conjunction to the ballroom but the chateau was huge. It had taken me nearly fifteen goddamn minutes to find the ballroom from my bedroom this morning. And that was after asking directions twice.

"Bring your coffee." He picked up his cup.

"No way. I almost pissed my pants yesterday, I'm not about to set myself up for a repeat performance," I declared and he laughed, the bastard.

The same monochrome gray, black and white room. The same uncomfortable antique furniture. The same fire burned in the grate. The same people sat in the same places all staring at me as if I knew anything at all.

All I knew was I wished I'd brought my damn coffee. I could smell Murphy's and it drove me crazy.

Councilor Celine Ducharme was dressed in olive green. It made her look a little like a very skinny, washed-out pea. Her shoes were nice, though. Christian Louboutin. Brown snakeskin peep-toes. In addition to crewneck sweaters, I had a thing for shoes. I might wear the same pair of jeans for an entire week, but I never wore the same pair of shoes two days running. I had to draw the line somewhere, didn't I? Of course I couldn't afford Louboutin shoes, at least not the real ones. I had a few pairs of knock-offs though—one really fabulous pair of black gladiator sandals with four-inch stiletto heels that were hell to walk on but worth the pain. Nobody could tell the difference except me, and with a short black skirt, I was hell on heels. In a good way.

"What are you smirking at?" Ducharme pounced on me as if I did something illegal when really all I did was stare lustfully at her Louboutin peep-toes.

"I like your shoes, Councilor," I said, because where else could I go, and was cheered a little bit when Murphy choked on his damn coffee.

Ducharme's scowl turned into a sleek smile.

"They are nice, aren't they? New. I just bought them on the rue—"
She brought herself up short and a bad-tempered gleam entered her eyes.

Allerton sat behind his steepled fingers but I swore I saw his shoulders shake.

The autopsy results were—surprise, surprise—inconclusive. They proved nothing but negatives. Rudi didn't have any pre-existing medical conditions. He had not been shot, stabbed or bludgeoned. He hadn't fallen and hit his head earlier in the day and walked around a living dead man for a few hours before succumbing to the fatal blow. He hadn't had an aneurysm or stroke. His heart had simply failed to keep beating and his lungs had stopped pumping air. The closest they could say was he might have ingested something poisonous but undetectable.

"Oh, for fuck's sake, that only happens in over-the-top far-fetched murder mysteries written by obnoxious English spinsters in the latter stages of menopause," Murphy complained with a derisive smile. "Undetectable poison my ass!"

Ducharme turned her beady brown eyes upon him with total disgust.

"Nevertheless, *monsieur*, that is what we are working with here, and again I ask you to stop swearing at me. I find it extremely offensive."

"I am not the most offensive thing in this room by a long shot, Councilor," Murphy shot back.

"I am not satisfied, either. I cannot help but believe Ms. Newcastle is at the bottom of this somehow. I beg of you, Constance, confess now and it will go well for you. Better than it will if we find out the truth and you kept it from us." Councilor Ducharme turned to me and I looked back at her but didn't say anything.

The grandfather clock chimed the quarter hour and I wondered how many more damn times I'd hear the wretched thing before I was able to leave the room.

"I want to go home," I heard myself say. There was a definite tremor in my voice that made them all look at me, most of them trying to mask their pity, which I didn't want or need. "Please can I just go home now? I didn't kill Rudi. I don't know what happened to him. One minute he told me my hands were cold, and the next he was dead, but I didn't do it. Just let me go home and I'll never come to a Great Gathering again. Ever."

The thought of sleeping in that tiny, cramped little box of a room for another night made me feel as if I were going to scream and never stop. The room we were in was small too. Too small for all of us crowded into it.

"Your hands were cold?" Ducharme questioned as if I had confessed something.

"From the water. The water bottles were on ice when the grandmother handed them to me. His hands were cold too, but I didn't care. I was going to bond with him. I was going to let myself fall in love with him, because I was tired of being alone without anybody, but I don't care now. I don't care. I'd rather be alone. I just want to go home. I don't like it here anymore."

"This is going nowhere." When Murphy's gaze met mine, I saw the pity there and the anger. "Let her go, Councilor. You can't prove anything and you know it."

"But that's just it. I can't let her go. I'm afraid I will need to keep her in indefinite detention until I am satisfied."

"Indefinite detention? What does that mean?" Murphy barked.

"Well, *monsieur*, English may be my second language, but I know it is your first and I believe we both understand to perfection what indefinite detention means. It means she stays with me until I know the truth."

"With you?" Murphy's lips peeled back in a silent snarl. "You're going to lock her up? Is there a dungeon in this damn place?"

Ducharme let out a trill of derisive laughter.

"You mock yourself at me," she accused, still laughing. "I will do nothing so barbaric. I simply won't let her leave. I can always use another servant. She can do my laundry. Shine my shoes. Make herself useful, but she will be supervised always."

The pulse in Murphy's neck throbbed visibly. The rest of him was frozen as if he were a statue with a working circulatory system.

"You're going to sit there and let this happen?" Murphy came to life then and swung accusingly toward Allerton. His Irish brogue was very much in evidence. "You've sat there all morning with nothing to say for yourself, but surely you've got something to say. You can't let her do this. You're on the Council too. You can't let her do this. She's Pack, damn you."

"Councilor Ducharme is the highest-ranking Council member here at this Gathering. I can't override her," Allerton said with real regret. He gripped the arms of his chair until his fingers turned white. He and Murphy stared at each for a long moment, both Alpha males, although Murphy was sorely outclassed and outranked.

Because he knew he outclassed and outranked Murphy, Allerton broke eye contact so he could look at Ducharme. They were more equally matched.

"What you object to is the fact that Constance is alone? Unsupervised?" Ducharme tilted her head to the side as she contemplated his words.

"For the most part, yes," she agreed. She flicked a speck of lint from her olive-green skirt and smiled to herself.

"But if she had someone to watch over her," said Allerton in a reasonable tone of voice, "such as a bond mate, perhaps? Then you would be satisfied?"

At the words *bond mate* Murphy looked up at the pale-gray ceiling and shook his head.

He shot me a knowing look and I shook my own head.

"Possibly, yes," Ducharme mused. She looked at Murphy and the most malicious grin ghosted across her lips.

"If I bond with her, you won't keep her as your indentured servant?" Murphy put it on the table and I winced. "You'd let her do that?"

"Let her do it?" the Councilor scoffed with a mocking laugh. "I would positively encourage it. Enjoy it. My only regret, *monsieur*, would be that when it came time for your own little fatal accident, I would not have the pleasure of telling you to your face I told you so."

The blood slammed to Murphy's cheeks. He'd shaved this morning and his skin was smooth. I remembered the feel of his beard beneath my fingers and saw Rudi's body convulsing. For a moment, I thought I might be sick.

"I'm almost tempted to do this so I can tell you I told you so, you little..." Murphy stopped himself from insulting her. Just. But Ducharme only laughed.

"Almost? That's what I thought. Constance, come with me, I'll put you to work right now. I have so many things that need doing, you understand."

"I didn't say no yet, goddamnit," growled Murphy.

I really thought I was going to throw up. My stomach did hideous things that made me wish the bathroom was a lot closer.

"Do I get a say in any of this? At all?" I wondered. I felt the sick sweat on my face but didn't wipe it away. I was afraid to move too much.

"Are you going to confess?" Ducharme's voice was saccharine sweet.

"I can't confess to something I didn't do. I meant do I get a choice between being your servant or his bond mate?"

"*Bien sûr.*" She shrugged. "Of course."

"You want to be her servant? Indefinitely? Which could mean for the rest of your goddamned life, Constance." Murphy spoke before I could, because he knew what I was going to say.

"No," I answered him. "I want to go home. But I guess that's not an option at this point. Walk away, Murphy. This isn't your fight. Just go away now while you can. I won't blame you."

He headed for the door and I waited for him to pass through it. Sweat trickled down the back of my neck and I hoped he had the time to shut the door before I puked. I also hoped Ducharme didn't move, because I thought I had a good shot at barfing all over her Christian Louboutins if she would just stand still.

He opened the door and was halfway through before he slammed it shut and beat a fist against it in impotent rage. "Everything that I know as a man, as Pack, tells me you didn't do it, Constance." His voice was barely above a whisper and he didn't turn around. He beat his fist against the door again, but not as hard as the first time.

"I didn't." I squeezed my eyes shut and tried so hard not to be sick. The fire burned so high it made the room sweltering. Oh, for an open window. For a breeze. For something cool.

"Bond with me." He turned around, his eyes very dark. "Don't let her win. You didn't do anything wrong."

"You don't even know what you're saying. You don't know me and I don't know you. We'll make a travesty of what bond mates are supposed to stand for. Get out, Murphy. Fuck you." I was perilously close to crying, but I was even closer to puking. I didn't want him to see me doing either.

"Fuck you, Constance. Don't do this!" His voice was harsh. "She'll make you into her dog. You want to be her dog? You want to wash her car and make her bed and shine her fucking shoes every day for the rest of your life just because you don't know me? That is a lie, because you know me at least well enough to know I can offer you a much better alternative than she can. And that I don't look down on you like you're beneath me, not as good as me, like she does. She thinks she's better than you are, and she'll make you lick her boots to prove it. Is that really what you want? Just because you were unlucky enough to be with that poor bastard when he died?"

"There was nothing wrong with Rudi. He shouldn't have died. Doesn't that make you even the least bit suspicious?" I was afraid to swallow the spit gathering in my mouth, but I would have to in a moment or risk drooling all over the damn carpet. This was hell. I was in hell.

"It makes me pissed off, that's what it makes me. I saw him with you. Laughing, enjoying himself. I thought he was just someone to fuck to you, and that what's you were to him, but it was more than that, wasn't it? You were going to bond with him and you'll lick her boots for penance for that, won't you? In his memory, because you couldn't save him. Well, that's a fucking bloody awful thing to do to a man's memory, Constance. The worst insult you could offer the poor bastard. Is that what you want to do? Insult the man, debase his memory, live a life of misery just because he's dead? If that's what you want, woman, you do it, but fuck you. I thought you had more guts than that, but maybe I'm wrong."

"I don't need you to save me. I don't need anybody to save me," I choked out then I was crying and I cursed myself for that. I'd rather have puked.

"I'm not trying to save you. Just give you a chance to save yourself. That's all. If you don't want it, to hell with you."

I didn't know what to do. The idea of spending the rest of my life being ordered about by Celine Ducharme was unendurable. But bonding with Murphy was hard to imagine. I didn't know him. He reacted against Councilor Ducharme's arrogance, but he might regret his offer to bond with me, and then where would we be?

For what seemed forever but was probably only a few seconds, I wavered between my two choices. Neither appealed, but one was definitely worse than the other.

Murphy opened the door again but closed it when I said, "I don't want to lick her boots. I don't want to do penance for something I didn't do. I'm not a martyr, damn you. You're serious? You'll bond with me? For real?"

I swiped at my eyes with the back of my hand, smudging my mascara all to hell, but I was beyond caring, even if I did look like sobbing raccoon.

"For real," he said. He was pissed off at all of us, and we cringed under his withering glare. At least I did.

"Okay." One little word put my life on a collision course with Liam Murphy's. I could not possibly be Councilor Ducharme's dog. Not in this lifetime, not in a thousand other lifetimes. I might not have murdered Rudi, but I damn sure would have been guilty of at least her attempted murder. Actual murder if I got lucky enough which, knowing me, I wouldn't.

Chapter 5

The bonding ceremony always took place the night before the last evening of the Great Gathering.

After I'd agreed to bond with him, the bastard had disappeared on me, and so we'd had no chance to discuss anything between then and the ceremony. I think he did it on purpose, because he thought if we spent any actual time together one or the both of us would change our minds.

Grey and I had been bonded at a Regional. I tried not to contrast that ceremony, not to mention the one we'd had with Elena, to this one.

Like everything else, it took place in the grand ballroom. I found it disconcerting that I could compartmentalize the fact that Rudi had died in this room, and yet, I could still eat there three times a day and now bond with someone. I tended to avoid the corner of the room where Rudi had died—everyone did—but we still spent a considerable amount of time there.

I suppose you couldn't rearrange an event for hundreds of people just because someone had inconveniently died in your biggest event space.

It was sunset, so I could look out the windows at the splashing fountains and not recoil in sun-blinded agony. I stood for a long time and gazed out at the water and sky. The water was a pale blue and the November sky was like an Impressionist painting of soft pastels—peaches, pinks, purples and a slight streak of palest orange. The clouds had formed in a puffed mass of white. Huge and majestic, like floating islands, and the sunlight spun them into cotton candy pink and lemon yellow.

They drifted across the sky in a lazy, unspecific fashion. A flock of geese fanned out in a V formation, honking so loudly I heard them through the glass. It was so beautiful I could barely breathe. I wished I had someone next to me to share the moment but I was alone.

The tables were set up for a party, with gold linen, the chairs swathed in purple fabric. The head table was set up for the Council who oversaw everything, and there were also tables for those who were bonding and their guests. The ceremony was not open to everyone—only to those who were bonding and their pack members.

It galled me to no end that because Councilor Ducharme was the highest-ranking Councilor at the Gathering she would be the one to perform the ceremony. But then this was a farce, anyway.

I wasn't allowed to go back to Paris, so at first I resigned myself to wearing jeans and a sweater. I'd done my hair and makeup with the other women in one of the fancy changing rooms, and they'd all stared at me, because there they were draped in beautiful gowns of every conceivable color and I had on a pair of pretty dirty jeans and a dispirited sweater. But my shoes were nice.

"Don't you have a dress?"

I looked up in the mirror and saw a young woman with strawberry blond hair and pale freckles sprinkled across her face staring at me with a most solemn expression.

"No," I said, but I smiled so she wouldn't think I was about to break down into tears, which I was, but not because I didn't have a dress.

"I brought two because I wasn't sure which one I wanted. Do you want to try on the one I didn't choose? I think we're about the same size." She didn't even smile.

I agreed to try on the dress, since I thought maybe if I did she'd stop looking like the world was going to end because I contemplated being bonded in a pair of Levi's.

The black dress was deceptively simple: sleeveless, *V*-neck, empire waist with one pleated ruffle from the waist to the hem that almost blended into the rest of the dress.

It fit and what was better it went with my shoes—a pair of black mesh pumps with a leopard print accent on toe and heel.

"I'm Constance." I introduced myself as I turned critically in front of the mirror, assessing whether or not the dress was too tight or just right.

"Sarah," she whispered, staring at me. Her dress was also black—also simple—only longer with no ruffle and a side slit along the thigh. Her shoes could have been more imaginative, just basic black pumps, but they were expensive.

"Who are you bonding with?" she asked.

I fingered the pleated ruffle and decided I quite liked the dress, especially since it showcased my shoes, which had been rather hidden beneath my jeans. "His name's Murphy. Liam Murphy." I had been going to wear my hair down, but I experimented with an updo, twisting it into a knot I held in place with one hand.

Sarah shrugged. "I don't know him."

Not surprising, but I wondered if that would be a blow to the man's ego to think someone hadn't even heard of him. He was front table material, after all.

Her accent was Australian like the couple with the twins at my table the first night. Maybe they were from the same pack.

Of course she wasn't wearing her name tag, not on her bonding dress.

"Mine's name is Lucas. Lucas Potter."

"Is he nice?" I asked, because she kept staring at me, obviously wanting something, but I was damned if I could figure it out. She smelled healthy, but not happy. She was certainly not a delirious giggler like three quarters of the room seemed to be.

"Not very," she admitted with an admirable candidness.

"Then why bond with him?" It fascinated me that somebody who had a choice would elect to bond with someone who wasn't very nice.

"My mum's making me. His dad. Our packs are combining. We're going to be the new Alphas and be the symbolic bridge." Her voice swooped with derision, and just for a split second, tears stood out in her eyes.

"On your birthday dump him. Sever the ties. Nobody can stop you," I suggested, and she gave me a grateful look and almost smiled.

"Mum says maybe it won't be so bad. But I don't like him. He's not very nice to the grandmothers and grandfathers, and that's never a good sign. He doesn't like kids, either, but that's fine with me. I don't want his kid. I hope I don't get pregnant."

"Sever the ties on your birthday. Go to every Regional you can get your ass to and find somebody else. Leave your pack." I said but in a low voice, because I didn't want everyone in the room to overhear, especially the one

I suspected was her mother. She had the same strawberry blond hair and their scents were closely aligned. She looked as if she were thinking about coming over to join the conversation. I wished Sarah would smile, but she didn't have anything to smile about.

"Mum says you're the one with that bloke who died before the Great Hunt. Was that you?" Sarah, like most Australians, was blunt.

"Yeah." I sat at the vanity table and waited for her to ask for her dress back, or at least walk away in horror. I was bad luck, and bad luck was like stepping in shit. It stuck.

Instead, she picked up a brush and brushed my hair.

"I gotta keep my hands busy, or I'll strangle my mum, I swear," she told me, her green eyes meeting my blue ones in the mirror.

She did a good job on my hair, pulling it up and pinning it in place, leaving some loose to frame my face. She did my makeup too before I did hers and her mother eventually joined us but we barely talked and, when we did, it wasn't about how unhappy we were.

Sarah introduced me as "Constance, you know, Mum, the one who was with that bloke who died before the Great Hunt. The German one."

You have to like Australians.

* * * *

Four women and three men gathered to bond at the ceremony. Sarah and I were forming duos, the others a triad.

We ranged in a long row together. We faced the Councilors who stood before the head table while our packs were behind us.

The room was lit by candlelight and by the fountains outside the window.

Instrumental New Age music, soft and evocative, played and I smelled food. There would be a feast after the ceremony.

Murphy had managed to get a suit—a black Armani with a purple tie to add a spicy dash of color. He was actually very handsome, more handsome maybe than Grey had been, but it had never been Grey's looks that had really attracted me—it had been his essence and his heart.

I didn't know Murphy's heart and I'd never experienced his essence. Maybe tonight, in bed, he would reveal that part of himself to me, but I didn't know.

We each held a small box. I'd picked mine out earlier. Lots of people brought boxes for sale to Gatherings, because it's a tradition to give your bond mate a box with the pendant he or she would wear after the ceremony. Boxes were made of wood or stone or *papier-mâché*. Once someone had boxes for sale made of matchsticks painted in bright colors.

The one I'd chosen for Murphy was made of tiny polished shells glued onto a small cardboard box. The shells were brown and cream and speckled. It had caught my eye among the other boxes made of wood. It had cost thirty euros, which wasn't much. Sometimes people would commission them, decorating them with jewels and gold and silver. Then they'd be expensive.

I sneaked a look at the box he held. It was metal. Pewter I think. I'd always admired pewter boxes. They were so old-fashioned, and they reminded me of the narrow streets of Boston. My birth pack was from a small town in Massachusetts. It was still there, but of course for the two years after Grey and Elena's deaths I had been isolated from them. My mother and father belonged to that pack, but we weren't close anymore. An investigation by the Great Council, even if you're ultimately cleared, doesn't do relationships much good and we had not been on great terms before that.

No one in my birth pack had come to this Gathering. It wasn't surprising. Mayflower, my birth pack didn't like to mix much. They were very self-contained.

Murphy and I stood shoulder to shoulder in front of the Council, but we didn't look at each other.

Sarah didn't look at her bond mate, Lucas, either. She stood beside me and I saw her keep her gaze fixed on the Councilor in front of her. Lucas stared at her, though, in a most possessive fashion. I smelled his greed and stubbornness. I didn't like what I smelled—at all.

On the other side of Murphy were the two women and one man making a triad. The man and his original bond mate were Belgian. The third woman was French. She was extraordinarily pretty and dressed in a burnt-orange gown. All three of them glowed with happiness. They were a good match.

The shells glued to Murphy's box were smooth against my skin. I ran my fingertips along their curling edges and wondered if he'd like the box, or even give a shit in the first place.

I knew my pewter box would be cold and not precisely smooth to the touch. There would be tiny bumps, small imperfections where the metal had cooled. I couldn't tell if the box was square or rectangular, because of the way he held it. I knew it wasn't round, nor, thank god, heart-shaped.

The shell box was shaped like a treasure chest with a domed lid. I wondered if I shouldn't have chosen a plain wooden box with maybe a few decorative insets of different types of wood. Maybe this one was too distinctive, too different. I wished I knew Murphy better but I didn't, of course, and I tried to be positive. Maybe in time we'd be a good match. Maybe we would.

Councilor Ducharme performed most of the ceremony in French and I followed along pretty well. Murphy had no problem, of course, nor did the triad, but Lucas scowled the entire time, pouting, and Sarah bowed her head and appeared to go somewhere inside herself.

If I'd been the one performing the ceremony when it came time for each of us to affirm we were doing this of our own freewill, I would have challenged Sarah. But Ducharme didn't. She barely deigned to do that part in English.

For the ceremony she wore her Councilor's robe—earth brown with a golden lining. Underneath it I saw she wore a dark brown dress, and I thought once she took off the robe she might look like a wafer-thin walking chocolate bar with blond hair.

The entire time she interacted with me and Murphy, she had a most insincere smile. But then so did we.

Murphy and I had to face each other to present the boxes. This was the part of the ceremony where it became free form and you could say what you wanted.

The Belgians and French woman were in tears as they exchanged boxes. Tears of joy and love. They embraced and kissed and helped each other put on their pendants, each with three stones. Then they were a triad.

I didn't say anything when I handed Murphy the shell box. It was warm from my hands and he ran a finger over the domed lid, his face thoughtful as he regarded it.

"How did you know I always wanted a shell box?" he murmured, but he was talking mostly to himself. He lifted the lid and took out the pendant. It was on a basic silver chain, one he could replace with something nicer if he wanted. It was long enough so he could put it over his head without unclasping it.

I'd chosen a peridot for the setting, but he'd supplied his own birthstone. It was a beautiful pearl. Maybe that's why, subconsciously, I'd chosen the shell box—an ocean theme.

I'd given up my peridot in its single setting and now when I opened the rectangular pewter box I saw it had been put into a double setting, paired with another lustrous pearl.

When a child was born, the mother chose a stone for her child. Modern fashion dictated that birthstones were chosen, but it hadn't always been that way. My mother had chosen my peridot and I would use it in every pendant I ever wore. Single when I was growing up, a double when I bonded with Grey, a triad when Elena joined us, back to a single, and now this double.

The pearl Murphy had chosen was large and almost perfectly round. Expensive. I'd chosen a nice peridot—not the biggest one that had been for sale, but not the smallest, either. It had a particular dark greenness to it that pleased me. My fingers had gone straight for it when I'd been shown a velvet tray full of jewels. As with the boxes, there were always people with birthstones to sell at Gatherings.

The pendant was suspended from a fine link silver chain that was nicer than the chain I usually wore by day. I unclasped it and Murphy watched me fasten it. He held the pewter box.

He wouldn't meet my gaze, and I thought that meant he was having second thoughts about bonding with me. We should be looking at each other instead of anywhere but. We should be smiling, laughing.

Ducharme watched us, her beady eyes full of acrimonious pleasure. Bitch.

Allerton watched us too. He smiled, but not with any malicious intent. He seemed genuinely pleased at our bonding. I couldn't understand why.

After the ceremony, we were shown to our tables for the feast.

Of course Murphy and I had nobody to sit with us, because neither of us had a pack.

It was a table for ten set for two. Pathetic, but at least I could watch the fountains.

"You're not eating much," Murphy said, his first words to me as a bond mate. Terribly auspicious.

I reached out for the wine bottle and refilled our glasses.

The food was delicious: game hen and a variety of vegetables, French bread and real butter, cheese, pâté, foie gras.

I choked down a few bites of the game hen and concentrated on my wine. It was red and it tasted like darkness tinged with chocolate.

There was lots of water on the table, of course, in case we wanted to shift later. I hoped we would. Even though I would have to explain my wolf, returning to wolf form regularly would be the best thing this bonding would bring into my life. I could almost taste the wind in my mouth.

I put my wineglass aside and drank some water.

"Those cookies look really good." I craned my neck to look at the dessert table nearby. "You want some?"

He nodded. A slightly relieved smile ghosted across his mouth.

As I pondered and picked over the macarons and other French cookies, I realized we'd sat in absolute silence for the entire meal, almost an hour.

"I've lived alone too long I think," I said, returning to the table with two plates—one piled high with cookies, the other with a huge slice of Black Forest chocolate cake. "I don't talk to myself. At least not out loud. Sorry if I ignored you during dinner."

"I'm not exactly talking your head off, either." His eyes lit up at the sight of the cake. Somehow I had known Murphy would like Black Forest chocolate cake.

I crammed a bright green pistachio-flavored macaron into my mouth and it melted on my tongue. I quickly followed with a raspberry pink one. Murphy attacked the cake.

"Where are we going to live?" I wondered, debating whether I wanted a lemon or chocolate-flavored one next. "Where do you live, by the way? I don't even know."

"Belfast," he answered. "Well, the outskirts, anyway. What about you? Boston, isn't it?"

"Yeah. I own a condo in the Brighton area. It's small but I love it." I chose the chocolate macaron and crunched it between my teeth.

"I've got a cottage," he confided. "Old but updated."

"Room for two? My condo's technically got two bedrooms, but the second one is tiny as hell. Office space mainly. You like Boston?"

"Never been," he admitted. "You've been to Ireland?"

"Ha," I said. Would he share just one bite of his cake? "This is the first time in my life I've been outside America."

"France," said Murphy in a disparaging voice. "You can't compare France to Ireland, Constance. Where do you want to live?"

"Well, I thought Ireland since that's where your pack is. It's a sure bet my old one won't have me back. Maybe we could keep my condo and visit Boston sometimes?"

"Sure," he agreed with a pensive smile. "About my former pack, Constance..."

He broke off then, because Councilor Allerton pulled out one of the eight empty chairs around our table and invited himself to sit down.

A waiter rushed over with coffee and brandy, and I went back to the dessert table to get Councilor Allerton crème brûlée. I got another piece of the Black Forest cake while I was at it and put it down in front of Murphy.

"Share this one with me?" I declared more than asked. He handed me a fork and grinned.

"I'm glad to see you two are finally smiling. I thought I was attending a wake instead of a bonding ceremony there for a moment." Allerton lifted his coffee cup and gave us a genial look before he took a swallow.

"The couple next to us weren't smiling, either," Murphy pointed out. He grinned a little to soften his words.

"Sarah and Lucas," I said. "Their packs are combining. They're the bridge. She just about hates him, and I don't know what he thinks, except I'm sure it's mostly about possession and very little about how she feels about anything. I told her to sever ties on her birthday and leave the pack. Screw them. She can find something better at a Regional. Or be alone for that matter."

"Not many of us do well on our own, Constance," mused Allerton. "I must say your counsel was not very, shall we say, diplomatic."

"I leave all that diplomacy shit to you on the Council." I shrugged. Murphy nearly choked on a bite of cake. He'd already eaten half of the second piece, the pig. I took a big forkful and ate it just to make sure I got at least one taste. That's when I understood why I never got any of the first piece.

"Holy shit, this is good," I said with delight. Murphy pushed the plate toward me.

"Nevertheless, Constance, in view of your own circumstances, I would be less inclined to offer advice like that in the future." Allerton didn't think anything I'd said was funny. He put down his coffee cup and glared at me as a ripple of unease slid down my spine.

I put my fork down.

"My own circumstances being what? Forced into bonding with somebody I don't even know? Or because everyone around me seems hell-bent on dropping dead?"

Murphy's face became shuttered and Allerton stared at me.

"You were not forced, Constance."

"Next best thing, Councilor."

"Would you have preferred the alternative?" His eyebrows drew together, and another shiver went down my spine. The cake and cookies sat like lead in the pit of my stomach.

"I don't see why she should be so unhappy. She told me her mother made her bond with Lucas. My mother never made me bond with anybody. I did what I wanted. We should all be able to do what we want."

"Well, that may be true, but life is not fair, Constance, is it?" Allerton leaned across the table and took me by the wrist. He gave me a little shake, much like an adult wolf would give a puppy. It was a warning. *Back off, little one.* "Sometimes sacrifice is necessary for the greater good, and rather than wallow and feel sorry and resentful for the sacrifices that may be required of us, why shouldn't we strive to be graceful about them? Rise above them? Make them work for us instead of against us?" He shook my wrist again. Harder.

"What is happiness, Constance? Our birthright? Or something we work for? Something we're rewarded with or something we are owed? The pack is made up of individuals, but there is also the Pack, is there not? The collective? The essence of every member bound up into one thing?

Rather than rot and die, Sarah's pack has chosen to align with another, a stronger one. And in doing so, they will survive, they will stay together and they will all grow richer for the association. Unless, of course, Sarah chooses to become a martyr and then the rot will grow and fester. The whole pack may dissolve, not just her original part of it."

I bit my lip and was silent. I knew I had a chip on my shoulder when it came to doing what was expected of me. My parents had been incredibly disappointed when I'd left to join Riverglow rather than stay with Mayflower. I'd been the fifteenth generation from the original Alpha pair, and from birth I'd been destined to be Alpha of Mayflower and produce the sixteenth generation. Instead, I'd thrown it all away on purpose. There were reasons and I still thought they were good ones, but it was always with me, the repercussions of my past decisions, which had been fueled by rebellion.

Chastened, I wondered if I had let my own past circumstances influence what I'd said to Sarah. Perhaps Councilor Allerton was right—I should have supported her in a different way and not fomented rebellion. How had it worked for me? Sure, I'd been very happy with Grey and Elena for a decade, but when they were gone I'd had nothing left. Perhaps if I hadn't burned so many bridges I might have had support the past two years.

"You were happy with Grey and Elena, I understand that. You were given a great gift, Constance, one you may never receive again. Ever. But will you spend your life mourning this gift, because you might not get it again, or celebrating the fact you had it at all?" He let go of my wrist and pushed back his chair.

"I wish both of you the best of luck in your bonding and I know you will do good things together, not because I wish it, but because of who you are. Good night."

He walked over to the table of Belgians and they made room for him, their faces growing solemn with the honor of his singling them out.

"I remember Gatherings where the closest I ever got to a Great Council member was craning my neck over a roomful of people and feeling awed if they even glanced in my direction," I muttered

Murphy snorted with laughter. "The problem with Council members is they are not all bark and no bite. They bite. And when they do, you mostly deserve it. Except that bitch from hell, Ducharme, of course. I have no idea what her problem is, and I hope I never find out." He pushed the cake plate back in front of me.

"Eat more, Constance. Don't let him ruin this for you. Dessert's been the highlight of your whole experience tonight. End it on a high note. Finish the cake."

I ate a bite because he wanted me to, but I really felt more like sinking into a hole and never coming back out.

After the food was cleared away, there was dancing.

Murphy and I watched, making sure not to look at each other and so be forced onto the dance floor together. My heart beat in a rapid rhythm against the tempo of the music, which continued to wind down, heading for the inevitable slow dance.

As if I'd summoned it, the lights dimmed even more and Madonna sang *Crazy for You.*

Oh, Rudi, I thought to myself. The man who sat beside me was a stranger and yet I wore his pendant around my neck. What had I done? What the hell had I done?

I must have made a sound, because Murphy leaned closer to ask what was wrong.

"Do you want to go up to the room?" I asked him, desperate to get out. If not for whatever had happened to him at the Great Hunt, I would be sitting here tonight with Rudi and Lucy and all their pack. And we'd be laughing together and happy. If Rudi and Lucy had sat next to me instead of Murphy this song would have been absolutely perfect.

Instead it was a freaking nightmare. I put my hand over my mouth and shut my eyes against the onslaught of grief that caught me by terrible surprise. It was almost as devastating as what I'd felt after Grey and Elena had been killed. I couldn't help thinking maybe I'd made a horrible mistake to bond with Liam Murphy. The damned song played on and on while Murphy sat there and stared, because he didn't understand me. Of course he hadn't been there that night when I'd danced to this song with Rudi. He couldn't know.

He smelled my despair—I saw it in his expression. His dark eyes were gentle and reassuring as he scanned my face.

"Come on." He touched my arm as he rose to his feet, and I felt absurdly grateful, because he didn't ask me what was wrong. I didn't really know myself. I followed him from the ballroom, leaving the music and happy people behind. Murphy seemed to know where we were going, which was good because I didn't. As we walked, I hoped someday we'd be happy together like the people in the ballroom.

Make the best of what you've got, Constance, I told myself. *Don't make this man regret his generous impulse. This is your new start. A second chance. Don't blow it.*

Chapter 6

"Wow," I said, doing a double-take when Murphy opened the door to the room we'd been given. All of us who had bonded tonight had been offered bedrooms in the chateau, and the one Murphy and I had been assigned was a far cry from the tiny little airless broom closet I'd been cramped in for the past two nights.

It was huge for one thing. The ceilings were massive and decorated with strips of gold. Two chandeliers glittered—one over the enormous bed and the other by the floor-to-ceiling windows. A sofa, two armchairs, a scrolled desk, a flat-screen television, an ornate bureau, gold draperies that fell to the floor in puddles of silk and a fireplace. A fire leaped behind a scrollwork screen.

An oval mirror adorned the center of the mantel and was tilted to take in every corner of the bed. Lothario would have been proud to call this room his own.

The attached bathroom featured a sunken whirlpool tub big enough for two.

"It's not heart-shaped, but what the hell," I called out to Murphy who prowled around the bed, his brow furrowed in a thoughtful manner.

Away from the music and ballroom, my equilibrium was restored. The grief and doom that had enveloped me like a shroud receded and left me with a feeling of near euphoria. I supposed leaping from one extreme to the next was hardly healthy, but I'd take the giddy high any time over the soul-sucking low.

"There's bubble bath, though. You want to take one with me, Murphy?"

I knew I was being forward, but the man was my bond mate and I had to start somewhere. Plus, Allerton was right. I was a spoiled little bitch and I needed to get a grip before I poisoned everything and everyone around me.

"Murphy?" I called his name again, because he didn't answer me. I went to the bathroom door and saw him opening the door to the hallway. "You going somewhere?" For what, though? There was champagne and lots of water and a bowl of fruit and even more macarons. We didn't need anything.

"I'll see you at breakfast tomorrow, Constance," he said in a strange voice and the door closed behind him.

"Breakfast," I repeated as if I'd never heard that word before in my life. The gloom tried to come back, but I wouldn't let it. Instead, a creeping numbness deadened my heart and head.

I took a bubble bath, anyway. Alone. And drank the whole bottle of champagne.

Woozy and with a slight feeling of unreality, I staggered naked to the bed and more fell on the damn thing than lay on it.

I was just about to pass out when I heard them outside. The Belgians and French girl. Howling. Shifted.

"Lucky bas'ards," I muttered thickly then I did pass out.

* * * *

The next morning was not pretty. I spent the first part of it puking into the regal porcelain toilet bowl next to the sunken bathtub. Then I took a shower in the tile-and-glass shower stall with the European rain shower head. Then I threw up again.

Someone had brought my clothes to the room and I put on my jeans and the sweater I'd worn for three days now thanks to the fact I'd been a near prisoner. Wet hair hanging in my face, I spent thirty-five horrible minutes trying to find my pendant.

I'd thrown it at the wall while waiting for the tub to fill. I'd have thought if a person threw a necklace at a wall and heard it hit it be would relatively easy to find the necklace the morning after. Especially when the curtains were open and the vile sunlight poured into the room like an invading army, illuminating every damn thing around except, of course, the necklace.

Eventually I found it tangled around the curtain rod. I had to stand on a chair balanced on the coffee table, then get up on tiptoe to reach it.

I broke the chain in the process, luckily not my neck. I found my regular one in the bottom of my purse coiled up in knots that took me half an hour to unpick.

To say I was rather late to breakfast would be like saying Columbus was rather late to India.

There wasn't even coffee left when I walked into the grand ballroom, Sarah's black dress over one arm. My hair was mostly dry, but still annoyingly damp, I had no makeup on and my head was splitting.

Murphy sat at the same table we'd shared the night before, a cold cup of coffee before him as he stared out the windows.

I didn't care that the coffee was cold. It was caffeine, so I took the liberty of separating the man from his coffee and downed it in one, heavenly gulp.

"No hair dryer in the room?" He took a good look at me.

"Don't ask." I set the cup down with regret and looked around to see if by chance there were any waiters carrying even a sip of coffee anywhere. All I saw were a few people lingering at their tables caught up in conversation or the last bit of breakfast. Most of the dishes had already been cleared, so the wait staff was probably in the kitchen loading industrial-sized dishwashers, or taking smoke breaks. The great urns of coffee had been removed as well, so I couldn't even get up and get my own cup.

"Last day of this damned thing. Where are we off to first? Boston or Belfast? What does your pack think? Our pack." That sounded weird on my lips. Nice but weird. "Do they do anything special when you join with your pack, or is it just no big thing? When can I meet them? Are there many of them?" I asked way too many questions, but my head hurt and I didn't want to talk about the night before, not that Murphy seemed likely to bring it up.

"Constance," he said softly, but it was enough to shut me up. "We don't have a pack. At least not at the moment. I'm working on it, though, so just give me some time."

"What do you mean? But they sent you here to find a bond mate, because they wanted you back." My lips felt numb, as if I'd put a grandmother's ointment on them, the one for easing pain by deadening sensation.

Why hadn't I realized this last night? They should have sat at the table celebrating with us. I ought to have been accepted into the pack last night.

Instead, we'd been alone at a table for ten.

Murphy's fingers tightened around the handle of his coffee spoon.

"They don't want me back, okay? Can we drop this now?"

I stared at him.

"You mean they don't want me. You're not the problem, I am."

"I said let's drop this."

"No!" My voice was shrill and he squeezed his eyes shut against the volume. I tried to modulate my volume a little but I shook I was so upset. "No, Murphy. We're not going to drop this. They didn't want me. Say it. Tell me to my face. I need to know."

"They don't want you," he said after a tense moment. Anger flashed across his dark eyes. "To hell with them, Constance, all right? I knew what I was getting into when I told you I'd do this, so to hell with them."

My head thumped queasily and I could taste burned coffee in the back of my throat as well as last night's champagne. It was not a good combination.

My fingers fumbled with the clasp to my pendant, I jerked it off and smashed it down on the table top.

"What are you doing? Put it back on." He kept his voice low so only I could hear him, but he was upset.

"No. You take yours off. Take it off, Murphy," I was humiliated. "We need to find one of the jewelers and get our own stones back and then you can go to your pack and tell them it's over with us. We need to sever ties now, because we only have forty-eight hours, otherwise we'll need to wait until my birthday and that's not until August, so screw that. I doubt you can find somebody else between now and the end of the Gathering, but there'll be a Regional soon somewhere and you can go there and—"

"Shut up and put your damn pendant back on." Murphy glared at me. He hadn't shaved again and the stubble on his cheeks and chin gave him an edgy, dangerous appearance.

"I'm not going to ruin your life, Murphy!" I almost shouted and he pounded a fist on the table, making the coffee cup rattle in the saucer.

"Will you shut the fuck up?" His voice was low, but venomous. "Ruin my life! Jesus God, woman, who do you think you are that you can ruin my life? And what are you thinking about saying we should sever the ties? You think Ducharme will shrug her scrawny shoulders and let you go back to Boston alone just because you bonded with me only to sever the ties not even twenty-four hours after? That's not what you agreed to, not what we all agreed to. And you said you didn't want to be her dog. Didn't I hear you say that, or am I going deaf?"

"It's not worth all the bullshit, Murphy," I argued, my chin wobbling. I was going to cry again and I wanted to smack myself. When the hell had I become such a baby about everything?

"I say it is, Constance Newcastle."

"Then why did you leave last night? You can't even stand to be alone with me in the same room and you want to stay bonded with me? I don't understand."

"Well, don't try to understand me. Just put your damn pendant back on." He heaved a sigh and looked as if he wanted to strangle me. "Besides, you don't want to walk out just before the curtain goes up on Act Three, do you now?"

"Act Three?" Now my voice wobbled just as much as my chin. I reached out for my pendant and he moved it closer within my reach.

"Act One, we were introduced by the mysterious Councilor Allerton and it was suggested we bond. We both declined, he laughed and rubbed his hands together like a comic opera villain and curtain. Act Two, all that drama with the old hag, Ducharme, the setup, the choice between indentured servitude, or a fate worse than death—bonding with me. Agony, indecision, some very dramatic speeches and we're bonded. Curtain, intermission. Now it's Act Three when we find out what he wanted us bonded for. Sure and you're not thinking he's some sort of half-assed Cupid, shooting arrows dipped in love potion at random unattached people of the Pack, are you now?" Murphy smiled, his dark eyes dancing as he looked at me.

"It wasn't a setup, was it? Rudi?" I was horrified and the smile died from his eyes.

"No, no, never go that far, but he used it. He used the situation. Turned it to his advantage. He sat there waiting for his opportunity with Ducharme. Hell, the two of them may have been in cahoots with each other. Maybe she never really meant for you to be her indentured servant, only to scare you into thinking she did. Nobody could believe for a minute you killed Rudi. Nobody in that room did believe it but her. And maybe she was playing along with Allerton. The point is we're just about to be propositioned. I thought he might have done it last night when he came to sit with us for coffee, but he's a sly one. He's letting the pot simmer just a little bit more."

"Ducharme meant it," I said with conviction. "I could smell that much. She might not think I killed Rudi, but she wanted me to crawl to her."

"So maybe Allerton used her too," Murphy said. "The bitch."

"How do I know you're not in on it?" I said doubtfully, which made him laugh again.

"Sure and are you really thinking I'd not be straight with you right off? Am I truly such a manipulative bastard as all that? Or are you thinking I'd never had a chance at bonding with you if it hadn't been a choice between that and something dreadful bad like Ducharme?"

"You don't want to be bonded with me," I said, unable to keep some of the hurt from my voice, which was stupid, because I didn't want to be bonded with him, either.

His eyes went dark and an unbearable sadness filled his face.

"That's not you, Constance. I didn't want to be bonded with anyone. I loved Sorcha so much, you see. I never wanted anybody but her, and if weren't for my pack hounding me, I never would have come here. Sometimes I wish I was an old grandfather and everyone would leave me the fuck alone."

"You never thought they wouldn't take you back, did you?" I kept going, because I had to, I had to.

"No." His mouth got tight. "That part hurt. I admit it. But it's done and I'm bonded to you and I'm not severing the ties. We both have to agree to it if we do it within the first forty-eight hours. I can't stop you from doing it on your birthday, but that's nine months away, isn't it? A lot of things can happen in nine months, can't they?"

I shrugged.

"Thank you, Murphy." I made myself look at him. His eyes were dark enough to drown in if I let myself. He was already starting to be familiar. I felt the extra weight of his pearl birthstone on the pendant around my throat. I could see the green peridot in his pendant wink in the French sunlight. "You didn't have to do this for me, and I know I've been really awful to you when I should be on my knees in gratitude. I keep thinking about Grey and Elena, and even Rudi, and comparing you to them and that's not fair."

"Why not?" His wistful smile told me he wasn't mad or insulted. "I'm comparing you to Sorcha."

"Oh, I'll never measure up to her."

"There is no measuring, because you're not her and it's completely different. I'm just saying, Constance, that we don't have to shove our pasts behind us and feel guilty about them just because they were wonderful. A little bit of feeling nostalgic, of feeling lost, that's only natural under these circumstances. I'm sorry I don't have a pack for you. I know you looked forward to belonging to a pack again. And you deserve one. If I have to start a pack myself, I'll get you one. You believe me?" He touched the hand I had on the table and his fingers were warm and strong.

"I'd say I'd find us one, but I somehow think you'll have better luck than me." I laughed, trying to make a joke, but he didn't smile.

"If you didn't walk around with a target on your backside, inviting people to kick your ass, they wouldn't, you know?" He took his hand away from mine and gave me an impatient glance. "I'm Constance Newcastle, I killed my bond mates. I know I'm not good enough for you to even talk to let alone let me into your pack."

I flushed.

"That's the message you're sending off. Loud and clear. I picked up on it the first night we met. That bitch, Mary, she was testing you. And you failed. Big time. Why don't you try defending yourself a little bit instead of rolling over and giving us your throat?"

"I did kill them." My voice was a guilty whisper. "I was driving the car. It wasn't raining. It was barely even dark. I wasn't drunk, but I'd had a couple glasses of champagne. I didn't know the car, because it was only the first day I had it and I drove it over the embankment and we crashed. Elena died on impact. She was in the backseat." I was crying now, but I couldn't stop talking. I wanted him to know. "She broke her neck on the back of my seat. The airbag saved me, but Grey was thrown out of the car. He broke his back in the fall. I got out of the car somehow and ran to him. There was blood coming out of his mouth and his body was all wrong. Twisted. I knew I shouldn't touch him, but I did. I wanted him to tell me he was okay. And he tried to. He always knew what I needed to hear. But he couldn't talk, because of the blood in his mouth, in his lungs. He clutched at my hand and his...his eyes. He was looking right at me when he died. Just like Rudi was. And I saw his essence leave his body and dissipate into the wind. Just like I saw Rudi's. I didn't kill Rudi. But I did kill Grey and Elena, and nothing you can do will ever make me say any different."

"Were they not wearing seatbelts?" Murphy asked. He handed me his linen napkin and I wiped my face with it.

"No, they never did," I said around the fabric.

"Well, he wouldn't have been thrown from the car if he'd worn a damn seatbelt. And she might not have hit the back of the seat if she'd worn hers."

"Oh, bullshit, Murphy. That's what Allerton tried to tell me too. Such bullshit. I drove the car over a cliff, goddamnit. Seatbelts or not, I shouldn't have done that."

A shadow fell across us and, with a flustered start, I recalled we sat in the grand ballroom where dozens of people milled around.

A tall curly-haired man stood looking down at us. His eyes were two different colors. The right one was blue, the left brown. The eyes were set in a handsome, very Irish face. He had on a Fair Isle sweater paired with tweed pants and his name tag said *Padraic O'Reilly, Mac Tíre, Dublin, Ireland.*

Mac Tíre was one of the biggest and most influential packs in the world.

"Paddy," Murphy said, a certain tension gripped his face. I realized they knew each other quite well.

Padraic said something in Irish and Murphy looked at me then answered in English. "Sure, I'll introduce you to my bond mate. Padraic O'Reilly, Alpha leader of Mac Tíre, this is my bond mate, Constance Newcastle. Constance, this is Padraic." Murphy's voice was sarcastic, his eyes very dark. A mocking smile crossed his face as he added, "Most people call him Paddy."

"My friends do, yes," said O'Reilly. He and I stared at each other. I was certainly not looking my best, but the way he gazed at me let me know in no uncertain terms that he found me very attractive. Heat sizzled between us—something raw and sexually blatant.

Murphy was pissed. His jaw tightened and his eyes became very narrow.

"You look like you've been crying. Has my man been saying something to upset you now? Sure and you aren't fighting after only one night in bondage." He laughed at his pun and broke our sizzling eye contact. Murphy scowled.

"I'm sure you're both upset at my decision about not letting you into the pack, but you'll not hold that against us, will you?" O'Reilly put a hand on Murphy's shoulder and Murphy shrugged it off.

I tried not to gape.

"Are you here to tell us you've changed your mind, Paddy? Because I can't think of another reason why you'd talk to me after what I said to you last night."

"You were angry last night."

"You're damned right I was. I still am. So unless you've changed your mind, fuck off."

I did gape then. Telling the Alpha leader of a pack as big as Mac Tíre to fuck off was almost like telling a Council member the same thing.

O'Reilly didn't get angry, though. He winced. The arrogant smile faded from his face and, for a moment, I saw remorse and frustration.

"Give us some time, Liam," he pleaded. "Nobody's sure of this woman yet. Give it a few months and then come back to talk to me."

"What? If I survive a few months you'll suddenly change your mind? You coward. You bloody coward. I'll never ask to join your pack again, Padriac O'Reilly. Got it?" Murphy was so angry one whole half of the ballroom could probably smell it. Most of them stared at us.

"Well, maybe I'll be asking you then," O'Reilly said wistfully. "But you'll have to wait. You'd do the same in my shoes, man. You know you would. You wouldn't let someone dangerous join our pack."

"No, I wouldn't," Murphy agreed, shoulders tense. "Constance is about as dangerous as that Fair Isle sweater you're wearing." He looked as if he wanted to spit at O'Reilly's shoes but he didn't.

"Let's agree to let time tell that tale, shall we? It was nice to meet you, Constance." O'Reilly gave me another one of his sizzling stares, but this time I refused to let it affect me.

"I wish the feeling was mutual, Mr. O'Reilly, but maybe time will change my mind. Anything's possible. Even homicidal Fair Isle sweaters I imagine."

O'Reilly burst out laughing and so did Murphy.

"Good one," said O'Reilly and there was something almost like regret on his face as he walked away.

"Can't take you anywhere," said Murphy. He sounded downright pleased about it.

"Mac Tíre," I declared. "Mac Tíre, Murphy. Only one of the biggest packs in the entire world. Maybe the biggest. There are over a hundred members of that pack alone!"

"One hundred and fifty-two. In Ireland. But who's counting," muttered Murphy.

"You. You were Alpha of Mac Tíre?" I said it as if it were an accusation.

"Once upon a time, yeah, I was," he agreed, a small smile playing about his lips.

"Counting one old grandfather inherited from Jonathan's birth pack, there are six members of the Riverglow pack. In our halcyon days when my triad was intact, there were nine of us. In my birth pack, which I thought was huge, there were twenty-four members. Twenty-five when I belonged. And you led a pack a hundred and fifty-two strong. Jesus H. Christ."

"It's just numbers, Constance."

"In Ireland?" I really heard what he said. "Oh, shit, that's right. Mac Tíre is throughout Great Britain isn't it?"

"Yes, but there's an auxiliary Alpha pair in each country. The Irish Alphas are only figureheads in those countries, for all intents and purposes. They just use the name, basically."

"Bullshit," I cried a little louder than I'd intended. Murphy grinned at me boyishly.

"I was Alpha for two years, Constance. Nobody's Alpha for longer than five, it's a rule. Got to let the women of childbearing age have a chance if possible, right?"

His grin dimmed a little when he mentioned childbearing. I thought of his bond mate dying in childbirth.

"Was Mac Tíre your birth pack too?" I asked.

He nodded, a shadow darkening his face.

"Why didn't you join a duo and become a triad?" I was honestly confused. Why wouldn't anybody with that kind of an option take it? And his pack was huge. He'd have had many different options.

"I told you. I never wanted anyone but Sorcha." Murphy's eyes burned bright with the heat of her memory. "Don't you get it?"

"I'm sorry. I'll shut up now." I was ashamed of myself for questioning him. His grief was so near the surface it wasn't fair to poke at it and stir it to the top.

"No, you need to know all this. You should know all this." He sounded more like he convinced himself rather than me. Instead of looking at me, he turned his head to stare at something across the room. Grief was stamped across his face. I wanted to reach across the table and touch him, offer him some sort of comfort, but when I did, he was up and out of his chair to go across the room and speak with somebody he knew. He didn't bother to bring me with him.

I found Sarah and returned her dress. She was no less morose than the night before, but confided Lucas was pretty decent in bed so she had that much at least.

Mindful of Allerton's words, I said little and steered the conversation out of the tricky depths of relationships and birthdays into safer ports.

When I walked away, I figured I would probably never see her again, and it was a sobering thought. So many times when you said goodbye you never really let yourself believe it was for the last time, but so often it was.

Lots of people hadn't bothered to come to the chateau for the last day—they'd stayed in Paris and gone sightseeing together. Rudi's death had cast a pall across the Gathering. It would be remembered, but not in a good way. I wondered if it were an ill omen to be bonded at a bad luck Gathering like this one had been. I thought of Murphy's face as he'd examined the shell box I'd given him. His bonding ceremony with Sorcha had no doubt been a joyous occasion—like mine had been with Grey and then Elena. Joyous was never a word that would describe our bonding ceremony—Murphy's and mine, but maybe there was joy in our future. At least I hoped so.

I looked for Roxanne, Lucy and Theresa, but I never found them. I wanted the closure and instead I got a vague sense of guilt of things left unfinished.

I sat on the stone steps of the chateau, enjoying the sun on my shoulders when I saw the hearse roll up. A side door to the chateau on the ground level, opened and four men carried a coffin to the back of the hearse.

I'd have thought there would be a back entrance to a place as big as a chateau. Maybe they could have waited to bring Rudi out when nobody was there.

Perhaps they delayed until his pack mates were gone, because they surely weren't there to watch his body being loaded into the back of the hearse. But I was there.

As the men struggled to shift the coffin into the back of the black hearse, I could barely breathe. I clutched my new pendant in both hands and couldn't help but think of a Louisiana cane field and a tall, gangly German boy who spoke barely any English but could kiss like a dream.

"Oh, my god, I just want to go home," I said through the tears that poured down my face. They were cold. It was a cold day despite the sun.

Murphy appeared from nowhere to sit beside me, his shoulder brushing mine.

"All you ever do is see me cry," I said with resentment. "I can do other things, you know."

"I know." His mouth tightened. "They picked a hell of a time for this."

"That's what I thought too. It's like they knew I was sitting out here."

"I think maybe one person in particular did," Murphy muttered.

We both watched the hearse drive away, tires crunching loudly over the gravel. The sun struck the chrome bumper and burned into our eyes.

When the hearse had pulled out of sight, I shifted on the stone step I sat on and looked at Murphy.

"When can we leave? Is there any reason why we're still here?"

"Just waiting on Allerton," he told me. "Maybe I was wrong, though. Maybe all he wanted us for was to bond, but I could have sworn there was something else."

I shivered and looked down at my shoes. The leopard print was scuffed on the toe of the left one. I scowled. I'd worn them too many times in a row. I wanted to wear boots, because my feet were freezing. I wanted socks. I wanted a new pair of jeans and another sweater, and I was tired of going commando, because I had no fresh panties. I'd managed to lose one of my favorite earrings and my watch was still in the broom closet room, which meant I'd probably never see it again. I was supposed to have checked out of my Paris hotel three-and-a-half hours ago and my passport was in the safe in that room, as well as all my luggage, including the stupid souvenirs I'd bought before this goddamn Gathering had begun. Souvenirs I'd been excited about bringing back to my tiny little condo in Boston, and now I could barely remember what they were. My tiny little condo in Boston was probably never going to be home again, because why would Murphy want to leave Ireland, and why should he? He'd already fucked up his life enough by tying himself to me, why should he have to give up his home too?

"Murphy?" I asked, sounding querulous. "What do hotels do with people's shit when they don't check out on time and they need the room for the next guest?"

"Constance, relax," he suggested in his *let's calm down the hysterical female* Alpha male voice of reason.

"No, you relax," I spat, even though he was not the one shaking and about to explode. "My passport is in that room and all my stuff, and I don't want to be stuck here while things are sorted out by a bunch of bullshit people in quasi authority. I don't speak very good French! I've been trying to get back to my room for two freaking days now and nobody will let me go. And now I'm late checking out and I don't even know where I live anymore and I'm tired and hungover and I hate France. I hate it!"

Murphy grinned and that only added fuel to my considerable fire of fury.

"I don't like France, either," he admitted with a conspiratorial wink. "So let's leave. Your passport is safe. All your luggage is packed, including your enormous collection of shoes. There were so many I thought you'd been here for a month, but I'm told you only had the room for a week.

That scares me because my cottage is big enough for both of us, but not five thousand pairs of shoes."

"I did not bring five thousand pairs of shoes to Paris with me," I cried.

"No, but I'm basing that figure on the dozen pairs you did bring with you. For one week. Which doesn't include the four pairs of new shoes I found still in their boxes that you obviously bought here. I had to use one entire suitcase just for shoes, Constance. Just. For. Shoes. Does that sound rational to you? Because it sounds bloody insane to me."

"You're a man. You wouldn't understand," I scoffed, cheeks burning.

"I wear shoes," he said reasonably enough.

I gave him a scathing look.

"You packed my things? Including my dirty clothes?"

"Especially your dirty clothes," he teased. "That's one of the things I did last night. I went to your hotel, packed up your things and checked you out."

"Can I have the receipt? I need to check my bank balance."

"No need for that. I paid for the hotel," he said. He waited for me to blow up.

"I'd rather you'd bought me a pair of Louboutin peep-toe pumps," I said and he completely lost it, laughing on the steps of the chateau like a lunatic.

Murphy had a rental car—a bright blue Renault—and all my stuff was in the trunk, including my four new pairs of Paris shoes, my souvenirs, dirty clothes and passport.

I was about to ask the bastard how in the hell he'd gotten the combination to the safe in my room, but just as I was about to open my mouth, Jason Allerton walked up the gravel drive to the rental car and stood there in the November wind, smiling genially at us.

The trunk was open, my stuff in various stages of disarray as I checked over Murphy's packing. I had my passport in hand, and Murphy stood nearby rolling his eyes as he tried to figure out whether he ought to laugh or be insulted by my inspection of his handiwork.

"Leaving?" Allerton shaded his eyes with one hand against the glare of the setting sun.

"Maybe in an hour, which is what it'll take her to pack all this crap up again. It took me two to pack it in the first place," Murphy commented and I almost threw my passport at him but managed to restrain myself.

Allerton peeked into the trunk of the car and seemed fascinated with the open suitcase full of shoes.

"Oh my," he said much in the same way someone else might have said, "Holy shit." Only he was a Councilor and Councilors did not say things like "Holy shit."

"I'm going to need to build an addition on the back of my cottage for her shoe collection," Murphy—the big mouth—remarked. "I hope I can get the permits. The cottage is on the historical register and they are particular about adding onto the existing structure. Maybe a shed out in the back garden."

"I'm not storing my shoes in a garden shed, Murphy," I warned him. "Especially my Louboutins."

"You haven't got any Louboutins," he said.

"Yet." I gave him a look and he gave me one back, and we both laughed.

Allerton regarded us fondly, like a father wolf watching his offspring pretending to be full-grown.

"You don't suppose you might have time for a quick drink or a cup of tea before you leave? You don't have a plane to catch, do you?"

Murphy grinned at me and I stuck my tongue out at him, because I faced away from the Councilor.

"No, I'd thought we'd spend the night in Paris. We're in no rush, Councilor."

"Excellent." Allerton beamed. He shut the lid of the trunk and crunched his way across the gravel back to the chateau.

I stuffed my passport in my purse and followed him, the wind whipping my hair around my face. I looked like a ragamuffin, I was sure.

Murphy's hair was tousled too, but he managed to pull it off much better than I did. His was shorter for one thing. Plus he wore clean clothes and looked altogether more respectable than me.

Allerton took us to a room on the ground floor. A dizzying array of priceless art was scattered about in a most contrived fashion. I was afraid to move lest I knock something fragile from the sixteenth century onto the floor and smash it to smithereens.

The sofa was stuffed with horse hair. I knew that, because Allerton told me. I think it was my expression of dismay when I sat and the cushions prickled my ass even through my jeans.

No wonder people from the olden days had such perfect postures. On furniture like this, you wanted as little of your actual body to touch it as possible. That meant sitting bolt upright, arms close to your sides...god forbid you use the armrest. That was for decorative purposes only.

We drank tea from paper-thin bone china cups with a faded pink rose pattern. I handled mine fatalistically, certain if I exerted just the slightest bit of pressure I would crush the handle. But if I didn't hold on tightly enough, the whole goddamn cup would slip through my fingers to crash on the floor and the tea would permanently stain the priceless Oriental rug I just knew wasn't made for walking on with stiletto heels.

Allerton and Murphy both handled the furniture and their tea cups as if it were no big deal. Some days it does not pay to get out of bed, I swear.

I was so busy trying not to break, spill, stain or slump I must have missed Allerton's opening lines in Act Three, scene two, but Murphy set his tea cup down onto its wafer-thin antique saucer, and said, "I noticed that too."

They both looked at me so I could either agree or disagree, but since I'd missed the original statement I shrugged.

"Yeah, you've been a bit preoccupied, haven't you," said Murphy and that made me grit my teeth. "But it's true, Councilor, attendance this year was way down from in previous years."

"I think people are nervous. There's a campaign of misinformation going on at best, I'm afraid. If you think you two are the only ones who have recent tragedies in your past, you are mistaken. There were at least a dozen people here this week who have lost their bond mates in similar situations. Accidents, but were they?" Allerton looked at us both and now I paid attention. I forgot about the paper-thin bone china and the way my stiletto heels left unfortunate dents in the Oriental rug. I even forgot about how itchy my ass was against that goddamn horsehair sofa cushion.

"You cleared me," I whispered. "I didn't cause the accident on purpose. I didn't."

All the blood seemed to rush from my head, leaving me feeling as if ice had been injected into the back of my neck through a particularly thick needle.

"No, Constance, you misunderstand," Allerton said quickly. "I don't think you did it. I think it was done to you. Somehow. That person you thought you saw in the road. Maybe he or she was there on purpose."

"There was no person. It was a shadow." I gulped. "Councilor, I've been over and over this. I think I wanted so much to have something to blame and maybe I..."

"Made it up?" Allerton finished for me. "Maybe you did. But maybe you didn't, Constance."

"I took the corner too fast," I confessed. Now my shoulders were as icy as my head, and soon I would be a block of frozen ice. "I didn't know the car. It was a Mustang, it had way more power than any car I'd ever driven. I'd never even driven a new car before, let alone one as powerful as that one."

I tried so hard not to think of that night, of going around the corner, the sudden realization I'd lost control. I think I hit the gas in a panic. There were no skid marks on the road. I think I'd hit the gas instead of the brake, because I was panicked when we went around the corner too fast and I felt the car go out from underneath me.

"And Rudi's death was too inexplicable, too extraordinary to accept and yet I saw the test results myself. I watched his autopsy and I did not see anything."

I stared at him, feeling myself growing progressively colder.

"I studied medicine, Constance," Allerton said, misinterpreting my stare. "Until I became a Councilor, I was a general practitioner."

"Murphy's bond mate died in childbirth. How could that be an accident?" I blurted then winced, because I continually managed to say hurtful things

"She didn't die in childbirth." Murphy's voice was flat, unexpressive. "She fell down the stairs at her lab. She was a chemist and she was working late and the lights failed, so she didn't take the lift, she took the stairs and fell down. And they didn't find her for hours."

"You think someone pushed her?" I had to put my tea cup down, because I started to shake.

"Nothing so crude. There was a power failure and the lifts weren't working. Apparently neither were the emergency lights in the stairwell," Allerton began.

"It was an old building," Murphy interrupted, his voice harsh.

"Stairwells are supposed to be kept clear, but someone left a box near the top of the stairs. The handrail snapped when she grabbed at it. Old building." Murphy's face twisted with an anger that was just as white-hot three years later as it had been that first night.

"Someone rigged the handrail, left the box on purpose?" I shook my head.

"It wasn't even an issue at the time, but it keeps happening, Constance," said Allerton. "Why do you suppose I came to investigate your accident myself rather than sending my Advisor?"

"Because Jonathan said I did it on purpose." I felt my own face contort with bitterness and betrayal. "He never liked me."

"I won't deny Jonathan petitioned the Councils, told them he thought you were responsible. He tried to say you were drunk, Constance, not that you actually tried to kill your bond mates on purpose."

"I wasn't drunk."

"You weren't given a breathalyzer test until much later. There was enough time for your system to metabolize any alcohol that might have put you over the limit. But you never denied you'd been drinking."

"Two glasses of champagne with a big huge piece of birthday cake," I snapped. "I wasn't drunk." I bowed my head. "But maybe I was impaired. I must have been."

"Constance, I don't think you were drunk," Allerton told me. "I came myself, because there have been too many of these strange accidents. I want you and Liam to get to the bottom of them. I'll help you all I can, but I'm a Councilor and everything I do is public. If someone is arranging all of this, they'll see me coming a mile away. But maybe not you two."

"You making us Advisors? Giving us some power?" Murphy asked.

"You can't be Advisors without a pack," said Allerton and something flashed across Murphy's face. "I want this to be as unofficial as possible. You'll have my cooperation. Behind the scenes. I'll give you access to the reports I've gathered. I've made copies and put them in the trunk of your car. The suitcase beneath the one with all the shoes." He gave me an amused smile and I smiled back, although I probably should have been a little offended.

"Liam, you've got money, you can afford to travel. You're looking for a pack, right?"

"Right," said Murphy. He and Allerton exchanged glances.

"Why does he need me?" I wondered. "Why couldn't you have just done this without me? What can I add?"

"I just said. Liam needs a pack. For you. But nobody's going to want you, Constance. You're poison, aren't you?" Allerton's face was sympathetic.

"Rudi was not an accident. Are you using that, or did you cause it?" I got to my feet and I wished like hell I could leave, because I didn't like what I heard and I didn't want to be a part of anybody's agenda, anybody who had anything to do with hurting Rudi.

"Constance." Murphy's voice was soft but compelling. "Sit down. Look at this man and tell me what you think. What does your gut tell you?"

I didn't want to but I sat. "He's not above using anything to advance his own agenda. You told me that much, Murphy."

"So I did. But do you think this man had Rudi killed just so you'd bond with me and provide me cover so I could investigate why a whole bunch of other Pack are dying in strange accidents? Do you think he'd do that?"

When Murphy said it, it sounded absurd.

"I don't understand anything," I muttered.

"I didn't cause Rudi's death, Constance," Allerton said and Murphy sucked in his breath, because Allerton did not have to say that. That should have been implied. Also, I should have been in trouble for even daring to suggest such a thing. "I'm tired of all these deaths. Always young people of the Pack. Innocent, outstanding people in our Pack who should have lived to be grandmothers and grandfathers. Who should have been Alphas and mothers and fathers, and instead are bones and dust. Maybe I'm growing old. Maybe I'm seeing conspiracies where there is nothing but grim reality. Maybe I'm afraid of growing old and dying and I'm trying to keep death at bay. I don't know, Constance, and because I don't know, because maybe I'm seeing things where there is nothing to see, I am asking you and your bond mate to help me."

"Maybe we'll see things too. We lost people and I know I want to make somebody pay for that," I admitted, fists clenched.

"I know. You've put yourself in that role, haven't you? Every day you blame yourself and punish yourself for driving that car that night. And you too, Liam. One of the finest Alphas Mac Tíre ever had and now you grow vegetables in the back garden of some small cottage near Belfast, and refuse to let yourself off the hook for not being there to keep your bond mate from tripping over that box." Allerton's eyes were fierce and furious as he talked, and I felt his power. He was strong. He was a leader. And he was so angry the entire room seemed to shimmer with his rage.

"But what if you could prove somebody else did it? It wouldn't bring them back, but you could stop that person from doing it to other people. Others of our Great Pack. You could have that much back. And you could forgive, perhaps, and go on. Let yourselves go on?"

"What if we don't find out anything?" I asked. "What if all we do is chase our tails round and round and round?"

"Well, at least you won't be filling your closet with shoes you'll never wear and growing vegetables you'll never eat." The Councilor's fury wasn't gone, just controlled.

Chapter 7

In the car on the way to Paris, I kicked off my shoes and tried to stretch my legs but the Renault wouldn't cooperate.

Murphy drove well. I didn't much like being in cars since the accident. I never got behind the wheel and I never intended to again, either. I took buses and subways mostly, taxis if I absolutely had to, but I managed to keep out of private cars as much as possible.

This Renault was the first car I'd ridden in, in more than a year. Since the realtor's car in Boston when I'd looked at condos.

I tried not to think about the fact I was in a car and instead picked up the shoe with the scuffed toe and turned it over and over in my hands, staring at it as best I could through the dashboard lights.

The sun had set and it was dark, windy too. The car buffeted back and forth on the road and I tried not to think about that, either.

Murphy and I had gotten into a fight earlier when I wouldn't fasten my seatbelt and he'd refused to start the car until I did.

Not a fight so much as a battle of wills.

I lost.

I think that bastard would have been perfectly prepared to sleep in that car rather than drive it, and I couldn't walk all the way to Paris. Not on stiletto heels. So I chose the lesser of two evils.

An hour in a car wearing a seatbelt. Or sleeping in one.

Murphy was still pissed off at me, because he wasn't talking. He'd called me a selfish bitch for not wearing a seatbelt.

"You have the damndest ways of giving tribute to your dead, you know that? It's pathetic and weak, and not particularly attractive!"

I hadn't said anything. I'd let him yell and rant at me while I sat there and debated whether I wanted to try to walk to Paris, and whether I wanted to do what Allerton had asked us to do.

I'd agreed to give it a shot, but that was because Murphy wanted to do it. I didn't think if I did find out somebody had deliberately caused my accident that it would in any way alleviate my guilt. Nothing could change the fact I'd been behind the wheel. Or had lived when they'd died.

"I think it's bullshit Allerton believes I buy shoes because I'm guilty," I remarked into the frigid silence between me and Murphy. "I bought lots of shoes way before the accident. You could ask anybody. I've always had more shoes than clothes."

"I think he meant that now you buy shoes to fill the hole in your life." Murphy unbent enough to talk to me. About five minutes after I spoke.

"Oh," I said, embarrassed. Then I got mad. "That bastard. Fuck him."

"I admit I grow vegetables so I don't have to think about anything," Murphy said. His voice was calm, reasonable—serene even—as if it didn't even bother him to be dissected by a Councilor. Did the man have no pride? Did anything sting him?

"And you really don't eat them? What? Are they poisoned with your guilt?" My voice swooped derisively and his face lit up with amusement.

"I hate most vegetables," he admitted. "I don't seem to grow the ones I do like."

"That is ridiculous, Murphy," I snapped.

"I know." He gave me one his boyish grins.

* * * *

I took one look at the hotel suite in Paris and said, "You have to be rich, Murphy."

It wasn't enough that we stayed at the Four Seasons Georges V. No, we had a two-bedroom suite in the Four Seasons Georges V bigger than my condo in Boston.

I looked at all the antique furniture and cursed silently.

"I do all right," he agreed. He tipped the bell boy, closed the door, bolted it and looked at my suitcases with a rueful grin. I'd insisted on bringing up all my stuff. I didn't want my shoes sitting in the trunk of a rental car all damn night.

"Traveling with you is going to be a bitch," he predicted.

I was secretly appalled at all my stuff too. I'd never traveled before. I had no idea shoes took up so much space in a suitcase.

"You can't be badly off yourself to afford a condo in Boston." he stretched out in a very pretty chair upholstered in cream-and-brown crewel-embroidered fabric.

Slouched in the chair like that, he looked downright cute. He definitely was an attractive man.

"I spent most of the money on the condo." I wandered around and gingerly touched some of the less fragile decorations. "Anyway, it was Elena's money, not mine. She was the one with the great job and the savings account. I had to spend it so Jonathan couldn't figure out a way to take it from me. Besides, a condo can be a home. It seems a lot less like blood money than a bank statement with a lot of zeros on the end that you're not used to seeing."

"The more I hear about this Jonathan, the less I like the bastard. I hope we don't run into him. I may have to punch his fucking face in just on general principle."

"It wouldn't take much to beat him," I said, making Murphy snort.

"Implying that even I could take him? You haven't a very high opinion of me, have you?"

"I don't know you well enough to have much of an opinion one way or the other."

"You hungry? Because I'm starved. Room service?"

"Room service? This is Paris, Murphy. We should be out in the streets, holding hands and looking in shop windows. Having dinner at an expensive four-star restaurant where the waiters appear at your elbow to refill your glass when you even think about taking a sip. Why would we order room service?" I wanted to go outside. I might have hated France, but I had a soft spot for Paris. Especially the shoe stores.

"Because I'm tired? We've got to be at the airport at eight tomorrow morning. Also, I thought we might start going through all this reading material Allerton gave us so we can plan our strategy and get familiar with things."

"What? You want to read case files on my last night in Paris? No way. Come on, take me out somewhere." I pulled open the curtains across the double windows and gazed down on the boulevard below. It was lit up for Christmas and full of pedestrians.

Picking up the hotel directory on the marble-topped coffee table, I read, "Marvel at the cuisine in *Le Cinq*, people-watch in the garden courtyard, or among the Flemish tapestries in *Le Galerie*. Hell, Murphy we don't even need to leave the hotel. We can eat at *Le Cinq* and marvel at the cuisine. We can see the Eiffel Tower from the terrace. I can't see the Eiffel Tower from the window and I want to see it."

"I don't want to marvel at the cuisine unless we marvel at it from plates brought up to this room, and I've seen the Eiffel Tower about ten thousand times and don't need to see it again." He sounded belligerent, which only made me dig my heels in harder.

"Pardon me for not living in Europe and having the Eiffel Tower just a daytrip away, Murphy."

"You go see it then. I'm staying here."

"I will," I threatened and he opened the suitcase Allerton had put in the trunk of the rental car and picked out a file at random. He settled back into the chair, turned on the light by his elbow and started to read.

"Oh, fuck this," I muttered beneath my breath then snatched up my purse and slammed out the door.

It turned out I wasn't dressed for *Le Cinq*, and the Eiffel Tower was not within walking distance, as my stiletto heels soon let me know.

I hadn't even gotten to the Seine before I had blisters, and all the magical possibilities of the night became more and more remote.

To get off my blistered feet, I went into a small café where everyone looked at me because I was alone. I sat down and tried to muster the courage to make eye contact with the waiter, because once I smelled food I was starving.

After I consumed a cheeseburger and French fries dipped in mayonnaise along with a cup of hot chocolate, I felt a little better.

The last of my stash of euros covered the bill, and after paying, I limped back out onto the sidewalk.

It was late and the shops were closed but I still window shopped. That cost nothing and it gave me a chance to rest my feet.

I made sure it took me at least an hour to get back to the hotel, and I had to stand in front of the elevators for a moment, racking my brains to remember the suite number before I could get on and press the right floor button.

I didn't have a key so I was forced to knock. That pissed me off. And so did the fact that Murphy didn't answer the door right away. I was just about to kick the damn thing and scream his name at the top of my lungs when I realized I could go down to the front desk and ask for a key. If I had the courage and could muster enough French, even though I was sure the hotel staff spoke English.

As I limped down the hallway, I heard the door open. Murphy stuck his head out into the corridor. His hair was tousled and he looked half asleep. I'd woken him, the bastard.

"How was the Eiffel Tower?" he enquired as I hobbled into the suite and viciously kicked off my stiletto heels. I picked them up and threw them into the trash for good measure. They were scuffed, anyway.

"Too far away," I snarled.

"You could have taken the Metro or a cab," he pointed out.

"I thought I could walk. I wanted to walk."

He followed me into the huge bathroom, which I thought was rude, but since I was only going to soak my damn feet in the tub I didn't bother to shove him out.

"So what did you do then? You've been gone three and a half hours."

"You can tell time in your sleep? Wow, impressive," I muttered as I twisted the gold-plated faucet knobs.

"I told you I was tired." He had the grace to look just a tiny bit embarrassed, but I was not impressed.

I debated rolling up the cuffs of my jeans, but decided to take them off instead. I forgot I was going commando but my sweater covered most of my ass and I didn't care. Why should I care? He was my bond mate, wasn't he?

He ducked when I threw my jeans. I had aimed for the corner, but he happened to be standing in front of it at the time.

The water stung my blisters. Two of them oozed a gross clear liquid and I grimaced, looking around for the soap. Piled on the counter by the sink were several small spa soaps wrapped in pretty paper. That didn't help, because the counter by the sink was a good eight feet away. My arms are long, but I'm not a giraffe.

"Can you get me some soap?"

He got me two bars and winced when he looked down at my feet. They were pretty bad.

"I hate France." I unwrapped one of the bars of soap. "And now I hate Paris too. When I first got here I thought it was cool they put mayonnaise on their French fries, but now I think it's disgusting. What do you put on French fries in Belfast, Murphy? Malt vinegar, right? You don't even call them French fries, do you?"

"Chips," he said in a soft voice.

"Ever heard of ketchup? Do you have it in Belfast?" I scrubbed at my feet, ignoring the pain. I didn't want an infection. Tomorrow it was boots and socks. And lots of adhesive bandages.

"I can get you ketchup, Constance. I can get you whatever you want."

"I highly doubt it." I threw the soap into the tub and water splashed all over me, getting into my eye. It stung.

"Sorcha loved Paris," Murphy said then. He got me a towel from the heated rack and handed it to me. "Restaurants and window shopping, all of it. I'm sorry, Constance. I didn't want to think about her tonight, but, of course, the instant you were out the door that's all I could think. When I wasn't feeling guilty about ruining the night for you."

I clutched the towel tightly between my fingers. I was such a selfish bitch.

"Why didn't you say? I'm the one who's sorry, Murphy. Jesus."

I stood on the bathmat and reached out to touch his arm, but he already moved for the door.

"I'm going to bed. See you in the morning," he said.

Appalled at myself, I took a hot shower and wrapped myself in a heated towel.

I thought maybe he would let me make it up to him, maybe he wouldn't make me sleep in yet another empty bed, but the door to the second bedroom was closed and he was behind it, I didn't have the courage to turn the knob.

* * * *

Murphy sat at the dining table—of course we had one in the suite—drinking a cup of coffee while reading *Le Monde* when I walked into the living room the next morning at a very ungodly hour compared to what time I'd managed to fall asleep.

The king-sized bed in the master bedroom had been too big. I kept trying to find the middle, but I never could, and then I had very fucked-up dreams on top of it all. But at least I wasn't hung over. Always a bright side, right?

"I had forgotten the joy of wearing panties." I grabbed a piece of toast from a toast rack and stuffed it into my mouth as I pulled my hair back and twisted it into a messy knot secured with a bright blue scrunchie.

Murphy laughed, which made me feel marginally proud of myself, considering what a bitch I'd been the night before.

"Do we have time for this?" I surveyed the huge breakfast with some skepticism—bacon, eggs, grilled tomatoes, croissants, pain au chocolat, coffee, orange juice and some diced up fruit in yogurt. "I thought we had to be at the airport by eight. It's almost seven now."

"I canceled our flight." Murphy flipped the newspaper over to the next section. He wasn't even dressed. He had on a pair of gray flannel pajama bottoms and a black t-shirt with some sort of Celtic design on it. Or maybe it was an abstract tree. "I figured we could read all these files and make plans just as easily from this suite as we could from my cottage in Belfast."

"But it wouldn't cost a thousand dollars a day in Belfast." I pulled out a regal-looking dining chair upholstered in nubby cream fabric.

"But I couldn't show you Paris from Belfast, could I?" He gave me one of his boyish grins and dared me with his eyes to protest.

I reached out for one of the omelets—the one with the vegetables. I had a feeling Murphy intended the one with meat and cheese to be his.

"Hey, is that ketchup?" When I saw the porcelain bowl full of a thick, reddish substance that looked remarkably like ketchup, I felt a surge of supreme happiness.

"Ordered specially for you. It helps this hotel caters to Americans." Murphy pushed the bowl closer to me and I doused my omelet liberally. He watched and I couldn't tell whether he was fascinated or revolted. I put a huge amount of ketchup-soaked omelet on my fork and raised it to my mouth. Bliss. Pure, American-tasting bliss.

"How about the Eiffel Tower? You want to go to the top with me? Race you up the stairs if you think you can do it." He reached out for the pain au chocolat and took a big bite while I washed the omelet down with orange juice.

"Can we read files on the top of Eiffel Tower?" I debated whether I wanted the remaining pain au chocolat on the white doily on the china plate.

"If it's not too windy, sure. You can do practically anything on the top of the Eiffel Tower, Constance. There's a restaurant, a gift shop and even a movie theater."

"Are there benches? Because if I'm going to read, I'm going to want to sit down."

Under the table he nudged my shin with his bare foot.

"Always so practical. That's one of the things I like about you, you know that?"

"Nice to know there's something," I murmured and he laughed. I was beginning to like his laugh.

* * * *

It was windy as hell on the top of the Eiffel Tower.

I'd known it was tall, but I took one look from the bottom of it and declared I was not taking the stairs, no way in hell, and so we took an elevator that was more like a cage, squashed in with a bunch of tourists. Most of them were German, and I wondered how long it would be before I could hear a German voice and not think of Rudi.

I cursed him, which was selfish of me, but I'd gone years and years living in America and hardly ever hearing German voices and now I lived in Europe and would hear German voices a lot, and I didn't want to think about him.

Murphy took me into the gift shop where I flirted with the idea of buying a beret, but in the end settled on a keychain with a tiny little Eiffel Tower charm on it. Murphy pronounced it the most goddamn touristy thing he ever saw and I shook it in front of his face, and said, "I am a tourist, Murphy. I am allowed to buy touristy things."

I clipped the keychain to one of the belt loops of my jeans, which made him threaten to throw his pendant into the Seine and disavow all knowledge of my existence, but I just laughed.

We found a bench and sat together armed with cups of coffee and two of Allerton's damned files.

While the rest of the people on the Eiffel Tower acted like tourists and looked down at city rooftops and the sweep of the river, Murphy and I read about dead members of the Great Pack. It didn't seem fair somehow.

My file contained the bare facts about a stockbroker named Grace Applebury, a member of a British pack in London, England. One Friday night six months ago, she'd gone to an upscale wine bar in Knightsbridge, had a few glasses of sherry, gone home to bed and never woke the next morning. She'd been thirty-eight, which in Pack terms meant she'd looked in her mid-twenties. She'd been autopsied and her blood screened by pack members and the results had been interesting. She'd had severe hemorrhaging in her cranium and a small contusion had been found at the back of her head.

Witnesses at the pub said she'd complained of dizziness and they'd thought she'd been drunk, but it was surmised that somewhere along the way from her home to the pub—she'd walked—she'd fallen and hit her head just hard enough to kill herself, but not hard enough for her to think she needed medical attention.

Had she been pushed? Knocked over the head? If so, why hadn't she said anything?

She'd been part of a triad with two men, who both professed to love her dearly, and neither one of them had a history of knocking her around.

Sobered, I sipped my coffee and tried not to let the November wind make me shiver too much.

Murphy moved closer to me on the bench, and lent me his body warmth. He didn't look up from his file until he'd finished and we traded. We didn't talk.

The second file concerned a forty-six-year-old petrochemical engineer from a pack in Sweden. A year ago, he'd apparently been drinking and ice fishing. He'd fallen asleep in his car and subsequently frozen to death overnight.

The only real mystery was that his blood alcohol level was not elevated very high. There was no reason to explain why he hadn't woken, or why he'd fallen asleep in the first place. Tox screens were inconclusive. He and his bond mate had been together for twenty years and were devoted.

Despite the pleas of the pack to join a duo and become a triad, she'd left the pack and no one was sure she would ever return.

"Twenty years," I murmured, and set the file down on the bench beside me. I drank the dregs of my coffee. It was cold. "Can I have some money, Murphy? I want more coffee."

He fished in his pocket and handed me a fistful of one and two-euro coins.

I went into the small café near the gift shop and bought us both more coffee, as well as a ham sandwich to share. We'd had a huge breakfast, but that had been hours ago.

Murphy sat slumped on the bench, legs stretched out, looking at the back of the *Musée d'Orsay,* or maybe the sky when I sat beside him. I handed him half the sandwich and one of the coffees and he flashed me a brief smile of thanks.

"*Le Cinq* tonight, or do you want to go out somewhere?" He took a swallow of coffee and closed his eyes briefly, as if pleased at the sensation of warmth in his throat.

"*Le Cinq* would be fun," I said, but I was okay with either. "Even room service. We can read more files if we order in."

"We're taking a break from reading files tonight."

And we did. We went back to the hotel after we finished our coffee and we read more files, but I had time to take a hot bubble bath and put on my black dress with the rhinestone straps. I accessorized with a pair of black patent leather pumps with rhinestone-encrusted heels and put my hair up.

While Murphy dressed I read a file about a twenty-seven-year-old computer programmer from Scotland who'd been in a car accident—drove into a tree. His bond mate had been paralyzed in the crash and had petitioned for and received permission from the Council to commit assisted suicide. One of the grandmothers from her pack had administered a painless but fatal poison and sat holding her hand as she died.

Pack didn't handle handicaps very well. People who were lucky had bond mates who cared for them, but if they didn't, they left the pack and looked after themselves. It was harsh and I hated it, but it was our way.

Pack could and often did commit suicide under those circumstances. Again, if they were lucky, they were assisted by their pack.

Murphy saw my face when he walked into the room and took the file away from me. "That was a bad one. I was going to keep that one aside. I'm sorry, Constance."

"I can handle this shit," I barked, but I wasn't sure if that were true. How many horrible, tragic stories did I have to read, and what was I supposed to get out of them afterward?

We didn't speak again until we left the room.

"What are the similarities you've noticed?" I asked Murphy in the elevator as we descended to the restaurant level.

He looked young and modern in a pair of gray pants and a darker gray jacket. His pendant was beneath a black shirt and black and gray tie.

I'd put mine on my evening chain. Peridot and pearl was not a combination normally seen. I saw Murphy studying my pendant in the elevator, but when I spoke, he said, "No. We are not going to talk about this subject during dinner. We're going to have a nice dinner, Constance. Promise me?"

I had zero problem with that.

We were placed at a prominent table in the restaurant, probably because we were staying in one of the larger suites, and treated like celebrities. I'd never had such an attentive waiter in my life.

We ate pheasant and foie gras and escargot in a deep dish pastry drizzled with herbed butter and we drank lots of wine.

Halfway through my crème brûlée and coffee, I leaned back in my chair, wondering if my dress was going to split at the seams. "Murphy, you know something, I like eating with somebody else at the table. I'd forgotten how much fun it is."

We'd laughed and joked all through dinner. He had a wicked sense of humor, Murphy did. The wine made his Irish brogue appear and I liked it.

A small shadow crossed his face. "Me too, Constance," he said and he looked so forlorn I was sorry I'd said anything.

I wanted to go back to the room. I wanted him to kiss me, and I wanted him to take my dress off and hold me flesh to flesh.

We did go to the room, but after he shrugged off his jacket and threw it neatly across the back of one of the dining chairs, he scooped up a pile of those damned files, and said, "Think I'll take these to bed and read them before I fall asleep. Nice bedtime stories, huh? See you in the morning, Constance."

He closed the bedroom door behind him and, sighing, I picked up the rest of the stack and took it to bed with me.

* * * *

We discussed the files over coffee and croissants at a café in the Marais the next morning.

We'd walked by common consent. I wore a pair of gray plaid Chuck Taylors and thick pink socks, so I was good to go.

The sky was overcast and heavy and we ducked into the café just ahead of the rain.

"So what do you think? What's the common denominator, if there is one?" I questioned as I greedily gobbled a croissant spread with honey while Murphy tried to guard his from my questing fingers and insatiable appetite.

He surrendered after two bites, because I was relentless, and allowed me to take what remained off his plate. It never even made it to mine. It went straight to my mouth.

"They were all young," he mused.

"How about their packs?"

"Small, medium, large. Some of them were popular members. Half a dozen of them were the Alphas, pretty equally spread between males and females."

"There was always someone left behind," I commented.

"It's a pack. There's always going to be someone left behind," he pointed out. The rain made streaks down the window we sat next to and cast intriguing shadows across his attractive face.

"Were they rich?" I wondered. "It doesn't say, but I remember thinking a lot of them had some pretty high-paying jobs."

Murphy elevated an eyebrow as he considered that. He wrote something down in a notebook propped open next to his coffee.

"The ones left behind, what happened to them?"

"A variety of things. Some of them made triads with existing duos, some of them left their packs, two duos and a triad were all killed together—the fire, the small plane crash and the carbon monoxide poisoning."

"It was never blatant murder," I said. "Even if it were an accident, the one who caused it was either killed or hurt badly. Except in my case. I walked away with a couple of scratches."

Murphy frowned.

"Senseless accidents. Many of them preventable but none of them malicious."

"They were all malicious if they were murders staged to look like accidents," Murphy said.

"Why? Why would anyone do this? And how could one person be doing this and not show up in the reports? Were there any of these that happened in the same pack? Or near each other?" The croissants felt heavy in my stomach and I wished I hadn't eaten them.

"Several happened to packs near each other. It's conceivable one person could have staged them. And maybe we're talking about someone who's Pack but doesn't have a pack. Free to move about invisibly. Nobody to care about him or her, or know where he or she is." Murphy pushed his coffee cup aside and stared moodily out at the rain.

"Or someone who lost somebody in an accident and was kicked out of their pack unjustly," I whispered.

Murphy turned back from the rain to look at me.

"I'd suspect you, only the files go back for five years and your accident happened two years ago. So unless you can tell the future and had a premonition I don't think I've solved the mystery quite yet."

"Someone like me, maybe," I pressed and he sighed.

"So what are we supposed to do, Constance? Ask Allerton to look through the Council files for a person or persons who lost their bond mates in tragic accidents and were somehow implicated and yet not convicted but still thrown out of their packs?"

"Why not?" I shrugged. "We've got to start somewhere. Give those Advisors who sit around on their asses all day making coffee for the Council something to do."

"Maybe what they'll do is gather a huge amount of files and dump them all at our front door for us to sort through."

I shuddered at the very thought.

The rain finally let up a couple of hours later and we splashed through puddles and took the Metro to the Louvre where we spent the entire afternoon not even thinking about those damn files.

We returned to the hotel just before dark.

That night I was all for room service, and while Murphy showered, I ordered it.

"Who was she?" I asked as we sat at the glass-topped dining table in our suite and ate steak and roasted potatoes with red wine. The bus boy had brought two crystal candlesticks with white tapers, and after he'd placed them on either side of a beautiful bowl of autumn flowers, he'd lit them.

I sat at the foot of the table, Murphy at the head. We were both in our pajamas and my hair was wet. He'd dimmed all the lights in the room so the candles were the brightest point of illumination. They cast dancing, circular shadows on the ceiling and made Murphy's face look mysterious.

"Who?" He stared at me, fork loaded with steak arrested just before his mouth.

"That woman. That brunette one," I clarified, but apparently not enough, because he set his fork down and gave me a quizzical look as he reached for his wine. He was obviously wondering whether I was about to throw a jealous hissy fit over some woman he might have glanced at in the Louvre and it was making him distinctly nervous.

I smiled maliciously. "The one you were with at the Great Hunt."

He relaxed his tensed shoulders, but only slightly. "Some woman," he said, clearly not sure whether we were going to have a fight, or even if he wanted to participate.

"Some woman? Did you even know her name?" I cried.

Irritation flashed across his face. "Of course I know her name, Constance. Sharo— I mean Karen. Her name was Karen." He'd had to search for it, and I rolled my eyes.

"You were contemplating bonding with this woman and you have trouble remembering if she was Sharon or Karen? Unreal, Murphy."

"Contemplating...what the fuck?" He gaped at me, steak forgotten in his astonishment. "Her name was Karen and I was not contemplating bonding with her."

"What were you doing with her then?"

"I would think that was obvious, considering the circumstances. I was going to have sex with her, Constance."

"What for?" I pressed and he continued to stare at me as if he weren't sure what language I spoke.

"What for? What do you mean what for? It was the Great Hunt. You need to shift for the Great Hunt and I haven't had sex for...a while now so I needed a partner." He shook his head. "Do you really need this explained to you?"

"Not really. I just wanted to know if you like shifting or not." I drank some of my wine and reached for the bottle. It was good.

"I really like shifting. A lot."

"Me too." I nodded. "I miss it. One of the things I thought I'd get out of bonding again is the opportunity to shift."

He sighed. "And you're finding it very difficult to shift when we both sleep in separate bedrooms, is that it? Is that what you're trying to say?"

"Well, the thought had crossed my mind, I mean it couldn't possibly be me, that's there's something wrong with me, so I figured you just didn't like to shift. But now you say you do like to shift, so I'm confused, because I refuse to believe I am that repulsive you'd prefer not shifting to sleeping with me."

"You want to shift? Is that it?" He shook his head.

"Eventually. At some point. Sooner rather than later."

Murphy picked up his water glass and drained it. He set it down and grinned.

"Okay, let's shift." He pushed back his chair.

"Now?" My mouth dropped open a little and I closed it with a snap. I'd really wanted to have sex more than shift, but somehow that had been difficult for me to admit. Now I was trapped.

"You did say sooner rather than later didn't you?"

"We're in the middle of the city, Murphy. We can't shift here."

"We don't have to shift the second we roll off of each other, Constance," Murphy said. "We have a car. We can drive to the countryside. It won't take that long. You can hold off the shift for an hour or two, can't you?"

"It's been two years. I'm not sure what I can do anymore," I muttered. I picked up my water glass and drank it all while Murphy stood and blew out the candles.

Before I lost my nerve, I wrapped my arms around his waist and kissed the back of his neck. He smelled like Armani cologne and red wine.

He turned around and pulled me roughly to him. His mouth crushed mine and I found out he could kiss spectacularly well.

I had on a bathrobe and a long t-shirt. He had me out of both in about four and a half seconds and I felt him hard against me as his mouth devoured mine.

But he wouldn't meet my eyes. Ever. We somehow got to his bedroom—it was closer than mine—and he got out of his clothes and joined me on the bed, but he wouldn't look me in the eyes.

He kept his closed when he kissed me, then kept them fixed to other parts of my body but not my face when we weren't kissing.

Once I tried to turn his face to mine, but he resisted my hand and so I gave up. I kept my own eyes closed and lay on my back with my face turned to the door.

After twenty minutes, I faked an orgasm just to make him stop and held him tightly as he came. I looked at his face then. His eyes were shut tight and I saw his lips move and I swear he mouthed her name. Sorcha.

Of course I thought of Grey too while we had sex. Mainly how much I missed him and how different sex was when the person you were having it with didn't love you.

I'd slept with Vaughn and Peter when I'd belonged to the Riverglow pack, but they did love me, as pack mates if nothing else, and we were good friends. They were my pack and we only slept with each other occasionally, like when the whole pack got together in the woods and shifted.

On the whole I thought I preferred separate bedrooms, after all.

I especially didn't want to shift after that, but I couldn't tell Murphy that. He was excited about it. I was the part to get over with before the real fun began. I'd always thought it was a more holistic experience, that the sex was just as enjoyable as the shift.

We didn't talk in the car as we drove to the countryside. I pressed my forehead against the window and pretended an inordinate interest in the scenery, and who the hell knew what Murphy thought.

I debated whether I should tell him that my wolf was a little different than most, but then I figured he'd find out for himself.

This is what comes of wanting to get laid, I thought with an inward sigh.

I didn't know why I worried, I had nothing to be ashamed of and so I put the idea out of my head.

Little by little as the city melted behind us and there were trees and stars and rocks and dirt, I felt her stir inside me.

My wolf.

It started as a strange lightness in the pit of my belly that radiated outward and lit me on fire, only it was cold and purple dark. My mouth filled with the taste of the earth and my ears, fingers and toes tingled.

I ripped off my Chucks and threw them in the backseat and Murphy started to laugh. He took a hand off the wheel and reached out to touch me, but I managed to move my arm at the last second so his hand fell short. I tried to make it look natural, as if I turned to look out the window rather than avoid his touch, but I didn't really care much either way.

My clothes felt tight, and while the fire inside was cold, I was hot on the outside. Burning up.

I shrugged off my jacket then sweater. It took me five miles, but I managed to wriggle out of my jeans too.

It was better in my underwear. I could take a deep breath.

"I don't want to go too much farther," I told him, and my voice was different. Lower pitched, sultry, wild.

He looked at me, gauging how close I was to losing control over whether I would shift and concluded I was on the edge.

When he pulled the car off the road, I was out the door before he'd turned off the ignition.

"Wait for me," he shouted, but fuck that, keep up if you could, asshole. Now he'd find out and I didn't care. My wolf had been silent inside me for too long, and the remembered joy of her being welled up until I felt as if I might split in half from the sheer exhilaration.

I ran until my legs were a blur. I saw rocks and trees, and through the gaps in the branches, the stars.

My ears felt as if they were scorching off, and when I looked at my palms, they had hair. Silver gray hair.

A grin of absolute delight nearly split my jaw in two and I threw back my head and howled.

Murphy howled back. He seriously lagged behind, the pussy. But then nobody could keep up with me when I ran if I had a big enough head start. In wolf form, I was uncatchable.

I splashed through a small brook and the cold water shocked me so much I fell down and that did it. I ripped off my bra and panties with fingers that were more claws and let the shift sweep me under.

It hurts to shift. It's not as bad as some of the movies project. My bones don't crack and my spine doesn't shorten—well, I suppose it does, but the shift is accomplished more on a meta level outside of this realm than here on the earth. It's as if I blink out into somewhere else as a human and blink back in as a wolf.

Sure, some of the shift occurs on this plane. Some fur, fingernails turn to claws. It hurts, but before it really starts to become horrific, I blink out.

Coherent thought changes after the shift. It's not so coherent. I forget my name but not who I am. Only I'm not who I am. I am Me. Wolf.

* * * *

Smell everything. Me smell Other. Friend. Friend? Know eyes. Like. Friend. Jump on Friend. Friend growl. Me no friend? This Me, Friend. This Me! Play with Me! Run with Me! Run fast. Run, run, run, run... Smell! Smell longlegs, little longlegs run over leaves. Eat longlegs. Him crunch. Smell! Smell dirt. Smell round thing from tree. Eat. Crunch. Friend! Smell Friend! Play, Friend! Play! Run, Friend. Run, run, run, run.

Oh, tired. Oh, can't run. Fall on grass. Smells good. Friend here. Friend warm. Friend lick Me. Cold on my face. Friend has good breath. Lots of smells. But Me tired. Me tired, Friend.

Put head on Friend. Friend soft. Friend breathes. In. Out. In. Out. Me want. Me want...something.

Me want.

Me cold. Me shiver. Friend warm. Friend hold Me. Fur gone. There is skin.

* * * *

I'm naked. No wonder I'm cold.

"Freezing." I burrowed myself close against Murphy's body. We lay on the grass. He was on his back, I was curled up against him, head on his chest. Our fingers were entwined and our hands were filthy. Covered with dirt.

"How the hell do you run so fast? Are you a cheetah or a wolf?" Murphy asked in an exhausted voice. He sounded kind of pissed. He was cold but sweaty. We both were. My clothes were back in the car. I always hated the part of shifting back when I realized my clothes were back in the car. Because I was never near the car and it was almost always cold. And I was always exhausted.

"I'm exhausted," I complained.

"Because you ran for I don't know? A year? A month? Six hours? I don't know. I can't keep track of time when I shift. All I know is you never stopped."

"I obviously stopped. We're not running now."

"You didn't stop, you collapsed."

"You kept up. I'm impressed." I went on the offensive and wriggled closer to him. He was cold, but I was colder.

Suddenly I remembered.

"You growled at me," I accused, going up on one elbow. It was on his stomach and that prevented him from answering right away. It also pretty effectively destroyed his desire to be anywhere near me, especially my elbows.

He got to his feet and headed back in the direction of the road. I rolled over on my stomach and was still for a moment. Crickets chirped in the bushes and above me the stars whirled in dizzying spray of glittering light. It was beautiful, but it didn't matter. My wolf might be a little rambunctious and not as focused and well-mannered as most, but that was no reason for his wolf to have snarled at her.

Murphy belatedly realized I wasn't following him and turned back.

"Are you coming?" he called, sounding impatient. It was too cold to be naked on the ground. Goose bumps pimpled my skin.

With a sigh I got up and walked toward him. He waited until I was beside him before he started to walk again.

"You didn't have to growl at me." My tone was haughty to indicate how offended I was and he grimaced.

"I'm sorry I growled at you." He didn't sound particularly sorry, and swore under his breath when he stepped on a rock. I nimbly avoided it and shivered as the wind picked up and blew my hair around my face until I was sure I resembled a witch. I felt like one.

"I don't understand why you did it, Murphy."

"I'm sorry I growled at you." He sounded rather like a martyr, and that pissed me off, because I was the victim,

"You think I should just ignore the fact you bared your fangs at me?" I elevated my eyebrows and swiped hair out of my face.

"I'm sorry I growled at you." He sounded like a CD with a scratch on it, constantly jumping back to the same lyric.

"You're not," I accused. We both shivered as the wind moaned through the trees, which showered us with dead leaves. What a goddamned gloomy night it was. His morose expression didn't help anything. "It's not nice to growl at people's wolves."

"I'm sorry I growled at you," he shouted. His hands balled into fists, and I was both proud and guilty that I'd finally provoked him. Through the trees ahead, I saw the car. Murphy had led us straight to it. The Pack always have a great sense of direction. I can't remember the last time I was ever lost. I might sometimes misjudge distances, but I always knew the way home.

"Why did you do it then?" I demanded.

"You weren't my pack," he said. Finally, a different answer, but this one really pissed me off. How dare he?

"Lame, Murphy. Lame answer," I had my arms wrapped around myself and I made little hops and jumps every few steps in the hopes that would stimulate my circulatory system and warm me the fuck up. "Just like it was lame to shift in middle of November when it's freezing."

"Doesn't it get freezing in Boston?" he snapped. "And it's not a lame answer, Constance. Just because you act more like a dog than a wolf doesn't make me a monster."

"A dog?" I stopped dead at that insult. "A dog? First I'm a fucking cheetah, now I'm a dog? Just because I wanted to play with you since you were a friend? I knew your eyes. That made you a friend. And bond mates are sort of a pack, aren't they?"

"You're not in my pack," he insisted, but his face was sad, or maybe that was the moonlight.

"Well, excuse me for the dog I am. I don't want to shift with you again. You're mean." I tried to make it sound like a flippant joke, but I was actually choking up, and in about five seconds I would cry. He didn't like my wolf. I'd been afraid he wouldn't and now it was confirmed.

"I'm sorry about the dog comment. You're not a dog." He tried to take my hand, but I evaded him and gave another hop into the air. "And I'm sorry I growled. I just...I— I'm used to shifting with my pack."

"You and Sorcha didn't shift alone?" I mocked, because I was so humiliated. He got angry.

"Leave Sorcha out of this discussion. In fact, let's not have it. Why do you have to analyze every last goddamn thing, Constance? So I growled at you. What does that mean?"

"You're honest and pure when you're wolf. Your true nature shines through and your true nature doesn't trust me. I'm a dog. I'm not Mac Tíre, I'm some fucking misfit from a tiny little misfit pack. I don't know my proper wolf manners. I'm too much. I run too much. I play too much. I'm just too much. I know, Murphy, you don't have to tell me. Jonathan told me a hundred million times. He and Vaughn and sometimes Callie too." I swiped at my leaking eyes and cursed that I cried yet again in front of this man. Finally it was out in the open. I didn't want to be ashamed of my wolf, because there was nothing wrong with her, but his reaction let me know he thought there was. With a keen sense of loss, I mourned for Grey.

"Did Grey tell you that you were too much?" Murphy's voice was soft and curiously soothing but I was still jolted. Could the bastard read my mind?

"No," I admitted as I eyed him warily. "But he...he was my bond mate. He understood."

"Well, I'm your bond mate now and I want to understand too. I do not think you're too much."

Fucking liar.

"Yes, you do. You do. You said so. I ran too much."

"I kept up, didn't I?" He gave me a boyish grin, but I didn't smile back.

"Murphy, the first fucking time I shifted, I spent the whole time screaming in what was probably supersonically high-pitched canine squeals because I was scared of this drum. This big huge drum that chased me, and the faster I ran, the louder it pounded and it wouldn't go away. You know what it was?" I swiped at my eyes again.

"No." He shook his head. "What was it?"

"My fucking heart," I said with true bitterness. "I was scared of my own fucking heart. I am a dog. Jesus."

He tried not to laugh. He tried so hard. But in the end he crumbled, and the next thing I knew, I laughed too.

"It's not funny. Goddamn you, it's not."

"It so is." Murphy had to stop walking and cover his face he laughed so hard.

I took the opportunity to shove him and he went down, but he dragged me with him and we rolled over and over in the cold wet grass, laughing and wrestling, until we stopped rolling and he ended up on top of me.

I waited for him to kiss me, but all he did was smile before giving me a hand up.

I had the sinking feeling I was never going to understand this man.

Chapter 8

The shower was separate from the tub in the suite. I took the tub and he took the shower. He finished cleaning himself before me. I really had managed to encrust so much dirt beneath my nails I spent a good fifteen minutes casting my mind back, trying to remember if I had been digging, and why in the hell weren't Murphy's nails as black as mine.

The memory of the rabbit flashed into my skull about the time I realized my skin was pruning and I sat in about six inches of filth. Poor rabbit. That's why my stomach felt the way it did and my breath was not minty fresh. It all fell into place.

Since Murphy was long gone, I took a shower after my bath and, wrapped in a towel, I made my way to his bedroom. The door was closed, the light off, and I could hear his heavy breathing. He wasn't exactly snoring, but it wasn't a romantic sound, either.

I said to hell with it and twisted the doorknob, and that's when I discovered he'd locked it. Feeling microscopic, I retreated to the master bedroom.

* * * *

Instead of a lavish breakfast spread, the next morning there were croissants, fruit and yogurt. And lots of coffee and water. No orange juice.

There was also a huge container of antacids.

I helped myself to a handful and crunched them up, telling myself I was not going to puke. I was not going to do it.

"Usually, I like French food, but I don't think I'll be ordering rabbit again anytime soon." I pulled out my chair and fell into it.

Murphy went a shade paler than he already was, but his lips quirked.

"I'm usually a little more finicky." He poured me some coffee. "But three years of thwarting that part of me definitely pulled away some of my usual control."

"I'm always like I was last night. I don't have any control when I'm wolf." I helped myself to a croissant, but once it was on my plate I stared at it instead of eating it.

"I'll work with you on that if you want." The offer was light, but sincere. He paid more attention to his water glass than me when he made it. I'd known our truce was too good to be true. Of course he wasn't going to let my wolf be what she was. He wasn't Grey who had always let me do what I wanted with her.

My jaw tightened. "I'm thirty-two years old. I've been shifting for twelve years. I don't need a teacher."

"Jonathan may have been a prick, Constance." Murphy reached for the antacids. "But he should have mentored you a little bit. I'm surprised Grey didn't do it."

"I told you last night. Grey understood me," I snapped. I pushed the croissant plate away and it clattered against the centerpiece of autumn flowers.

"Just a little control, Constance," Murphy said in a soft voice that pleaded for me not to blow up on him. "Believe it or not, it makes the experience all the better." He crunched up a handful of antacids. "Especially the morning after."

I thought about the uncomplicated joy of being wolf, of the wind in my face and run, run, running everywhere, full of the sort of profound happiness that I never, ever felt anywhere else. I supposed I was like a child when I shifted, and maybe Murphy was telling me it was time to grow up. I was too much. Everybody had always told me that, but I'd been too stubborn to listen, Grey and Elena had indulged me. But they weren't here anymore, Murphy was. And he wanted to work with me to help me gain control. The man had bonded with me to save me and the least I could do was work with him. He was not going to indulge me like Grey and Elena had. We did not have that sort of bonded relationship. He'd given up a lot for me. Maybe I needed to give back, or I'd end up alone again. My wolf would lose either way, but at least if I worked with Murphy I stood a chance of belonging again.

"All right," I said, but my face must have reflected something of my sense of loss, because his own became shadowed.

"That wasn't like you. Not even a small skirmish, let alone an epic battle?" He pushed my croissant plate back in front of me but I had no appetite.

* * * *

We went shopping after breakfast. He brought me to dress shops and five different shoe shops. I tried things on because he seemed so eager for me to do that, but I didn't like anything. I didn't want anything. All I could think about was my wolf and how I might lose her. How I would betray her when all she wanted to do was run, play and be with her friends.

There was a Christian Louboutin shop on the rue de Grenelle, and Murphy chuckled when he saw it and gave me nudge toward the door.

"I'll buy you any pair you want, Constance. Go on. You've always wanted Louboutins, haven't you? Here's your chance."

I went in but even the lure of feathered peep-toes and studded gladiator sandals couldn't puncture the poisonous cloud of self doubt and grief that suspended me within its depths.

I wished I'd never come to France, or decided two years was long enough to be alone. What was wrong with being alone, anyway? Now I wanted to be in Boston, walking along the Common, watching the lovers, because I wouldn't envy them at all. Not even a little bit.

Surrounded by six boxes and twelve shoes, Murphy asked me which ones I wanted. I knew if I said I didn't want a pair, he'd be more upset than he already was. He tried not to show it but he was awfully angry at himself and he shouldn't have been, because he was right. I was irresponsible and immature, and he was only trying to help me.

I pointed at random and ended up with a pair of grey metallic peep-toe pumps in a water snake pattern. They were gorgeous. And expensive.

Murphy didn't even wince when the clerk told him the total was nearly eight hundred euros. He paid and joked around in French.

Outside in the sunshine, I lifted my face to it and decided I needed to stop being such a baby. I didn't want to be alone, and maybe he was right. Maybe my wolf would like to work with his. If I didn't at least try I would never know. "Thanks, Murphy. I'm hungry. Do you want lunch somewhere maybe?"

His face lit up when I spoke to him and he brought me to a small brasserie nearby that served wonderful quiche. We drank an entire bottle of white wine between us, which I thought was rather decadent for one in the afternoon, and when we walked back out onto the sidewalk, the sun had disappeared. We hadn't taken more than twelve steps before the sky split open and a deluge gushed down.

Parisians and tourists scattered. Murphy grabbed my hand and we dashed for the Metro, plunging down the steps into the artificial light below.

"Can't get your Louboutins wet," he teased as he bought us tickets at the counter.

"They're in a bag," I pointed out, but I was secretly relieved to be out of the rain. They were very nice shoes. Nice shoes? Hell, the nicest shoes I'd ever, ever had.

We managed to find two seats together on the train and I sat by the window, clutching my new shoes to my chest.

"You're not wearing your pendant," Murphy commented. I put one guilty hand up to my throat and encountered only bare flesh. I'd taken it off the night before and put it carefully into its pewter box because I was going to shift. I never wore jewelry I wanted to keep when I shifted, because I always lost it.

"I took it off last night and I guess I forgot to put it back on this morning. I'm not used to wearing it," I confessed. "I never wore it much these past two years. The single setting, it was like a reproach somehow. I'll put it on when we get back to the hotel."

"I thought you might be mad at me."

"Murphy, if I were mad at you, I'd tell you to your face. I wouldn't be so passive aggressive as to not wear my pendant and leave it to you to figure out I was pissed. Besides, you know me. I can't keep my anger contained. You'd know it. You'd know it in a second." I laughed, wanting him to laugh too. He was so worried when he didn't have to be.

"I don't want to change you, Constance." He stared very hard at the back of the neck of the old man who sat in front of us. "Jaysus, you're only one of the most fascinating people I've ever met. I don't want to change you. I just want to help if I can. Which is a joke, because I can't even help myself, can I? Buying you Louboutin shoes and telling myself that will make it up to you, the fact that I insulted you and, worse, hurt you, because you think I want to change you and the truth is I'd like to be more like you."

"They are very nice shoes, Murphy," I said and the ghost of a smile quirked his lips. "Nicer than Councilor Ducharme's. Mine were about two hundred dollars nicer than hers."

"You gonna wear them tonight when I take you out to a club?"

* * * *

We danced a lot at the nightclub. My Louboutins looked fabulous. I looked fabulous. Murphy looked fabulous. I had one of the best nights of my whole life.

We got back to the hotel around three in the morning after a hilarious cab ride where I tried to speak French, and Murphy and the cab driver talked over themselves correcting me and we laughed when we all but fell through the door.

I tripped over one of his feet and he had to catch me, because five cocktails and four-inch heels are not necessarily a very stable combination.

His eyes darkened with desire the second before his mouth came down over mine. We hadn't kissed at the club, or even really touched, but we were all over each other in the hotel.

He took me to his room where I kept on the Louboutins but lost the rest of my clothes.

I thought for sure he'd look at me this time. He'd initiated it, after all. But he didn't.

I wanted it to be real. I so desperately wanted it to be real, so I pretended I was her. Sorcha. I let myself do the things I thought she would do, and he still didn't look at me, but it didn't matter, because I'd found a way to make it work.

And when he said her name just before he came, or mouthed it because I didn't exactly hear his voice but I did read his lips—that worked too. Because I was her. At least for that moment.

Afterward he rolled over, his back to me, but he kept his body in contact with mine.

I rolled over too and after a moment I felt his arms steal around my waist and he burrowed closer. I kept my eyes shut and tried to pretend I was her, but it didn't work. I was just me again.

Chapter 9

"I still feel it inside me," Murphy declared. He was on his second cup of coffee and the middle section of *Le Monde*. I was still working my way through a plate of scrambled eggs liberally dosed with ketchup.

I knew what he meant—he felt his wolf inside him. We hadn't shifted last night, but we still could tonight if we wanted. Our wolves were still awake inside us but not for long. Twenty-four to forty-eight hours, usually.

"You want to shift? Finish your breakfast and shift?" His dark eyes challenged me and I swallowed my mouthful of eggs, and asked, "In the daytime?" It wasn't precisely an alien thought, because we could do it, but it was unusual.

"Why not? We'll drive out to the country again and do it."

"Are you going to mentor me?"

He folded the newspaper and set it aside. "Only if you want me to."

"Shouldn't we work, Murphy? We haven't in two days." I wasn't precisely turning him down, but I wasn't sure I was up for being mentored, and while he said it was up to me, he'd be disappointed if I said I didn't want him to start teaching me how to behave in wolf form.

"We'll work tomorrow. Our flight leaves at ten thirty for Houston. We've got a whole day to do anything we want."

"Houston?" My eyebrows elevated. "Like in Texas? That Houston?"

He nodded, grinning.

"What's in Houston?"

The grin faded.

"An accident. Allerton called me while you were in the shower. He wants us to investigate it."

* * * *

Just the thought that I was going to shift was enough to wake my wolf inside me. She hadn't been sleeping, she'd been dormant, waiting her turn, but she knew it was close and once again in the car I had to take off my shoes and my shirt and ride the cold fire inside me until Murphy finally pulled the car off the road.

He let me run, get a head start, but I heard him behind me. I could also hear his voice in my head as I replayed his words during the drive.

"I'm going to do things you probably won't like, Constance, but please don't shut down on me after we shift back. Please try to understand. You came from a small pack, and discipline doesn't matter much in a small pack, but it matters like hell in a bigger one. You have to know how to follow. You have to know how to submit. Haven't you ever been on a Great Hunt at a Gathering or a Regional?"

"I only ever went to two Great Gatherings. One when I was eighteen and not old enough for the Great Hunt and then this past one. My pack couldn't afford for us to go. And at Regionals I was always with Grey and Elena and Vaughn. The four of us would go off on our own."

"They'd follow you, you mean."

"Maybe. Probably. It's never been an issue before."

"Just try not to take this too personally. You want to be Alpha someday. You've got to know how to follow before you'll know how to really lead."

But I didn't want to be Alpha, only I couldn't tell him that. He was Alpha.

The sunshine felt like melted gold dust on my skin. I could smell it. Tangy and fresh. Warm like butterscotch only not as sweet.

I collapsed on a bed of pine needles and soft earth. The trees made a canopy above me and I heard a crow cawing and couldn't understand what he was saying but I knew he didn't like the fact I was there.

My wolf strained inside me, clawing to get out, whining and yipping, wanting to play...

* * * *

Me play. Play. Me run. Me smell Friend. Run, Friend. Run...Friend growl. Me play. Friend growl. Friend snap, sharp teeth. No. Me scared. Me run. Me...

* * * *

I stared at the sun and it hurt me. I put an arm over my eyes to shield them and I smelled blood. There was blood on my arm. Blood under my nails.

I sat up and I was alone in the middle of a field of golden grass. It was cold but the sun was warm and there were scratches on my legs and blood under my toe nails.

"Murphy!" I shouted his name, because he wasn't there.

The sun went behind a cloud, making everything gray and obscured, and I shivered, wrapped my arms around myself, buried my face in my knees.

The scratches on my leg and my arm itched. Throbbed.

I got up, took a step and fell down. I lay face down in the golden grass and smelled rain in the clouds above and the gray sky tasted like wet newspaper in my mouth and nose. I didn't like it. I wanted to go home.

Murphy found me. I don't know how much time had passed, but it seemed like forever.

He had my clothes and a first aid kit, and before he let me get dressed, he wiped the scratches on my arm and leg with something that stung like hell and made me want to hit him, but I held still.

He had an accusingly white bandage wrapped around his left bicep. Blood seeped through it.

"I bit you," I said, horribly ashamed of myself. It had gone worse than I'd ever imagined. I'd broken Pack rules. You didn't bite. You play bit. You feigned. But you never *really* bit.

He nodded, concentrating on the three long parallel scratches down my right thigh. They oozed blood but they were not very deep. Neither were the ones on my arm.

"Your wolf made her so scared. So mad," I whispered as he smeared some sort of topical gel on the scratches and they started to go numb.

"My wolf just wanted yours to roll and show her throat, her belly. She wouldn't do it," he remarked, his gaze fixed on his work. "I didn't expect she would the first time."

"Did you expect her to bite?" I felt like shit. Like a monster.

He looked up and gave me a brief smile.

"No," he said, ripping off a piece of gauze bandage.

"Why didn't your wolf bite back?" I tried to help him, but he pushed my hands away. My nails were shredded, encrusted with blood and dirt.

"She ran too fast to catch. Even on three legs." He ruffled my sweaty hair and picked out some pine needles and leaves from the snarls.

He offered me a steadying shoulder for support while I put on my jeans. I wanted to cry when he buttoned my shirt for me, because it was so oddly intimate but I didn't.

"Are you thinking coherently when you're in wolf form?" he asked. We had to walk slowly because of my leg.

"I think in broken thoughts. In simple words. I feel more than anything."

"Because you never tried to do anything different," he said.

* * * *

No matter how high I pushed the heat in the rented Renault, I couldn't get warm. The sun had vanished, taking with it all the autumn warmth and leaving behind only bitter November cold.

Shivering, I pulled the zipper of my leather jacket up as high as it would go and craned my neck to look in the backseat for my scarf.

Murphy had a wet sheen of sweat across his upper lip that he wiped away with the sleeve of his jacket. He looked at me and I wasn't sure whether he would complain about the heat, or tell me how worried he was about me.

"I don't want to be tamed," I raged. I wanted to shout, but my jaw shook too hard for me to raise my voice much. "I like running free and not thinking coherently. I like the purity and the simplicity. You want me to think and I don't want to. I think enough in this form."

"If we join a large pack, Constance, they'll make you change, or they'll sever the ties." Murphy tried to sound reasonable, but I sensed how impatient he was with me. His arm hurt and I smelled fresh blood.

"I think you might need to go have your arm looked at," I said. "Do you know anyone in a Paris pack? We need to find a grandmother."

"You and your grandmothers and grandfathers. You quote them to me, you rely on them to fix things, but why did none of them in your life ever teach you how to be a wolf?"

"I don't need to be taught something that comes naturally!"

"We are not natural, Constance! We are not wolves. We are Pack. There is a difference. We have consciousness and we have control and we are not simply creatures of instinct and senses. We have an obligation to ourselves, to the Great Pack. It's an honor and a privilege, not an escape. Not a place to play and forget yourself, but a place to work and find yourself. Why did the grandmothers and grandfathers never tell you this?"

"Maybe because I'm supposed to work it out for myself?" I guessed shrewishly. "Maybe because I never shifted with a grandmother or grandfather before."

"I'm sure you didn't, because they would have made short work of you. I went easy on you, but I won't again." Murphy cast a dark look at the blood-soaked bandage on his arm.

"I'm not going to shift with you again," I decided and he made a sound very like a wolf's growl.

"I asked you not to take this personally, not to shut down on me, Constance."

"You're not taking it away from me. The one thing I have left, my wolf. You're not taking that too. I won't let you."

"I haven't taken anything from you. I'm trying to give you things."

"Things I don't want." I looked mutinously out the window. "And you have taken things away from me. My pride, Murphy. My self-esteem."

"Oh, bullshit!" Now he was really angry. "Don't give me that crap. If you were any kind of a wolf, you wouldn't lose your pride and self-esteem so goddamned easily. I didn't take those things from you. You threw them away, because you have no idea who the hell you really are. You play a good game, but you can't win it."

"Leave me alone!" If the car hadn't been going seventy miles an hour, I would have jumped out. I didn't want to be in a car. I didn't want to be in France. I didn't want to be with him.

"Now I see why Allerton wanted us together. He wants me to fix you."

"I am not broken!" I screamed at him. "I'm not broken! Maybe he wanted me to fix you, you bastard, you ever think of that? Maybe he wants you to let go a little bit. Just a little tiny bit. You have to always be in control. You have to always analyze everything and intellectually understand it before you even halfway allow yourself to experience it emotionally. You let yourself love Sorcha and now she's gone and that's it for you. You went there once and you're not going back again. Well, fine, don't. Live in your climate-controlled prison, but don't expect me to lock myself up too. I want to be free. I want to feel things!"

His face was dead white and he gripped the steering wheel so tightly I thought his fingers might break.

Every time he thought about her, every time he heard her name, he smelled the same way. Like grief and loss and complete annihilation. He did feel. For her, he felt. And all his intellect could not make the hurt any less that she was dead and lost to him.

I had to bring her up. I had to rub his face in the fact she was dead. He tried to help me, and I knew I needed it, but I would always lash out in defense of my feelings, then think about what I'd done afterward.

We were a match made in hell, Murphy and I. Damn Allerton. Damn him.

"I'm sorry," I whispered as we drove into the city. It was raining. Droplets of icy water dotted the windshield but Murphy didn't turn on the wipers. He didn't even acknowledge I'd said anything.

He pulled up in front of the hotel and waved away the valet.

"Aren't you coming in?" I blinked at him stupidly and he shook his head.

"Just get out and go up to the room. I'll be back later." He didn't look at me.

"I said I was sorry," I whispered.

"Go on," he snarled.

The bath water stung my scratches. I pulled off the bandages and soaked in the water until it turned a grungy brown. I took a shower and washed my hair three times, but I could not wash away my guilt.

Four o'clock on a November afternoon in Paris is a dreary time. From one heartbeat to the next, there's a strange tension. Nothing to do but think, and at four o'clock, your thoughts get all tangled and anxious. Even if you pace the room in your bathrobe, rolling the sash between your fingers, stopping to look out the window at the boulevard below your window then pace again, your thoughts never really calm down.

I heard him come in around eleven. I was in bed but not sleeping. I'd ordered room service for two and it was still cold and uneaten on the table. I hadn't touched anything, had in fact, been sickened by the smell of it, and had retreated to bed but sleep was elusive.

I heard him get into the shower, heard the water gurgle down the drain. I could smell the metal in the water, I could smell blood and dirt and sweat.

My face to the wall, I waited to hear him go into his room and lock the door against me.

My door wasn't closed. It was open—a silent invitation, one I knew he wouldn't accept but I had made it, anyway.

What's worse than being alone? Being alone with somebody else.

I tried to evoke memories of Grey and Elena, of the three us snuggled together under the covers on a cold winter's night, me in the middle, because Elena hated being boxed in and Grey liked to sleep with one leg on top of the covers. Safe. Warm. Loved.

But for the first time Grey and Elena wouldn't come to me. They crumbled to pieces in my head. Little bits of them fell off and faded away. Maybe someday I wouldn't have anything left except a vague sense that they were ever there in the first place.

The water shut off. The bathroom light went out. The mattress sank under his weight as he lay beside me. I couldn't move. I was afraid to. Afraid if he knew I were awake he'd leave.

"I'm sorry too," he said into the darkness. His arm stole around my waist and he burrowed closer to my body. I still couldn't move, but at least now I could sleep.

* * * *

Hands caressing me eased me out of the dark dream world. Lips on the back of my neck. Sleepily, I murmured his name and tried to roll over into his arms but he wouldn't let me.

His hands and his mouth roused me, a slow, delicious desire that became more and more intense.

He slid into me from behind so I couldn't see his face and he couldn't see mine. We moved together slowly but ended up on our knees, him behind me, me bracing myself against the fabric headboard of the bed.

He had my hair pulled back tightly, I felt him breathing in my ear, panting. Maybe that was me.

When I came, I screamed, I couldn't help it, and he laughed in my ear—a sound of triumph. He bit my earlobe, making me shudder, and said, "This one, at least, you didn't fake, did you now?"

I should have known better than to fake anything with him. He's Pack. He knows.

Chapter 10

Flying business class kicked major ass. It beat the hell out of coach.

It was only my second time in a plane in my whole life.

Murphy let me have the window seat and I watched, fascinated, as we hurtled down the runway, going faster and faster. I felt her inside me, my wolf, she was excited because we were going fast and she adored speed.

My ears tingled and I had to sit back in my seat and squeeze my eyes closed to keep her from waking any more than she already was.

Beside me, Murphy put his hand on my knee and I was grateful for the touch. It grounded me somehow.

Champagne and orange juice, my pre-flight beverage of choice, sloshed around in my stomach. I smelled jet fuel and the heavy floral scent of the perfume the woman behind us wore. I heard Murphy's heartbeat, steady and slow, and my own, faster, lighter.

Then we were airborne and leveling off, and when I opened my eyes again, there were puffy white clouds everywhere and I couldn't see through them. We were very high and the sun was bright above us, making the clouds so white and defined I thought I could reach out my hand and come away with pieces of them clutched in my fingers.

The flight attendant walked by and wanted to know if I wanted something to drink.

I had another champagne and orange juice. What the hell.

It was about ten hours from Paris to Houston. We did it non-stop. The food was better than that of some of the cafés and brasseries in Paris. Served on china plates. The coffee was the only thing that didn't quite measure up. I put some brandy in mine and fixed the problem.

It was still early afternoon in Houston when we arrived. It was nearly Thanksgiving, but the moment I stepped outside and followed Murphy to the rental car desk, I was uncomfortably hot. It had to be at least eighty degrees. Maybe more.

The first thing I did was take off my leather jacket. The sweater I wore underneath went next. The thin cotton shirt I wore beneath the sweater was about right for the temperature, but it was much the worse for wear after ten plus hours.

The trees all had leaves still, most of them green, and there were swimming pools everywhere.

Murphy drove us to a small boutique hotel downtown. Hearing American accents again threw me off. I'd only been in France for three weeks, but America seemed like Mars now. I didn't like the feeling.

I'd never been to Houston, so this wasn't my territory. The American accents were not the New England ones I was used to. They were slower. The desk clerk called Murphy *darlin'* when she checked us in. She had very big hair, white teeth and a tailored blue dress.

Murphy flirted with her while I stood there sweating with my hair in my eyes and the taste of too many glasses of champagne on my tongue. I didn't much like Houston.

Our room was soulless compared to the hotel rooms in Paris. It was a suite, but with only one bedroom.

I found the bed almost as soon as I put down my suitcase. I hadn't slept on the plane. I never could sleep on planes.

The pillow smelled like lavender. Murphy pulled the heavy draperies across the window and I heard him prowl around the suite, then I was asleep.

* * * *

"Y'all really ought to work on your timing, you know that?" The Alpha male of Dark Bayou, the Houston-based pack was a thin, tall man between the ages of thirty and forty. He had unruly brown hair, steely blue eyes and wore a pair of jeans with a Houston Astros t-shirt. His name was Bobby Jenkins.

We stood in the living room of his house, which was not in Houston but in a town called Katy, and it seemed composed mostly of strip malls and parking lots.

The house had an open foyer and a staircase leading to a second story, which was also open. Two skylights streamed sunshine down upon us. I saw Murphy's eye lashes and the stubbly specks of his beard. He looked tired but sexy. He wore a black button-down shirt with the sleeves rolled up to his elbows along with a pair of jeans and Red Wing boots. An expensive silver wrist watch gleamed from his wrist. His pendant was tucked down the neck of his shirt.

In France he hadn't seemed so Irish, but here, where he did not fit in, he appeared very foreign.

Bobby Jenkins seemed suspicious of him. Murphy picked up on this, and if anything, the Irish lilt in his words became more pronounced.

Air-conditioning blew through vents near the ceiling, making me wish I'd worn a sweater instead of the thin, light purple t-shirt I had on. Air-conditioning in November seemed wrong somehow and it contributed to my own growing sense of unease. The whole place reeked of grief and confusion, and I wanted to leave in the worst way.

Murphy seemed unaffected. He stared around the house as if it impressed him when I was sure it did not.

Bobby Jenkins's bond mate, the Alpha female, was in the kitchen making food. There was already a lot of it on the huge dining table. The living room and dining room were combined into one big room with an L-shape where the table was.

Funeral foods were on display—casseroles and cheese and crackers, olives, pickles, and something that smelled a lot like seafood.

"Crawfish etouffee." Bobby Jenkins followed my gaze to the covered dish on the table. "My bond mate's from Louisiana. Help yourselves." His invitation lacked real warmth, and he kept casting looks at a small woman in a green skirt and black t-shirt that really didn't match. She had long, brown hair that fell into her face, because her head was bowed. Her shoulders shook with suppressed tears.

"Kevin went and drowned himself in the goddamn hot tub two nights ago and this is a real shit mess, so I'm sorry if I'm not exactly thrilled to see y'all." He pushed a hand through his hair and I understood why it looked so unruly. "Molly won't stop crying and Jolene won't stop cooking. And I've got some goddamn Advisor from the Regional Council asking all these goddamn questions and...hell." He pushed his hand through his hair again and gave us a small half-defensive, half-apologetic smile.

"How'd y'all end up here in Houston wanting to know about this pack?" His eyes became shrewd all of a sudden, because it was weird that an Irish man and a New England woman would show up on his Houston doorstep, wondering if the pack were interested in two more members.

Murphy smiled. It was a diplomatic, friendly smile. One he probably practiced in front of mirrors, because it looked sincere and the man was about to blatantly lie.

"We met at the Great Gathering, Constance and I, and we knew at first sight we had to be together." Murphy put his arm around me and pulled me close, and I pretended to melt into him. To be malicious, I drew a finger down the side of his face. He never let me touch his face, he always turned away. But he couldn't let Bobby Jenkins of Dark Bayou see him reject me. Not if we kept to the script.

He didn't turn away, he reached out and took my hand with his and gave the palm a distracted kiss, never taking his gaze off Bobby Jenkins.

I took my hand back and managed a bright smile.

"She wants to stay in America and I'm looking for a change, so we thought we'd wander around the States for a while and check out prospective packs. We're on our way to New Orleans next."

Bobby Jenkins nodded but suspicion lingered in his eyes.

"Do you mean Kevin drowned himself on purpose in the hot tub?" I blurted, because I was increasingly aware of the way Murphy's fingers were gently stroking my hip. He was such a bastard.

Acute irritation washed over Jenkins's face.

"What the hell?" he drawled. "You're like that Advisor, you know that? He asked the same damn thing. Why would he do that? He and Molly were happy, and he'd just bought a house—next door to this one, y'all ought to see the game room. He's got a seventy-inch flat screen television and a Wii and...aw, hell. No, ma'am. He did not drown himself in the hot tub. We'd been drinking and I guess he fell asleep. Mindy found him next morning."

He looked out the sliding glass doors to a small terrace where a little girl of about ten was having a tea party with a group of dolls and stuffed animals. She was not smiling.

"Mindy's his daughter. His and Molly's. He was Alpha before me."

Amy Lee Burgess

His bond mate, Jolene, a buxom brunette with snapping dark eyes and jangly earrings blew into the room then, laden down with a plate full of fried chicken.

Her energy was enormous and she reeked of grief and cooking oil.

"Y'all want some chicken?" She thrust out the plate, and I think if we'd declined, she would have burst into tears.

We each took a piece. I nibbled on a leg and my eyes went wide with appreciation. From the sizzle on my tongue, I think she put hot sauce in the batter. It was the most astoundingly delicious fried chicken I'd ever put in my mouth.

Murphy had a breast and he too looked surprised at how good it was. I think he had been prepared to be repulsed by Southern cooking. Elitist bastard.

Bobby gnawed on a thigh.

The atmosphere in the house was choking and I wanted to enjoy my chicken, not strangle on it, so I took another leg and some napkins and escaped out the sliding glass doors. The little girl poured pretend tea from a bright pink teapot decorated with Disney princesses into a bright purple tea cup, also decorated with princesses. The doll behind the tea cup was a lady doll—curly blond hair, an expressive china face and realistic sapphire eyes that open and closed. The eyelashes were stiff and bristly. She wore an old-fashioned silk dress that had once been canary yellow and now was more cream with age. She had to be at least a century old.

"She's very pretty," I remarked.

The little girl had dark hair and even darker eyes. She had the most solemn expression I'd ever seen on a ten-year-old's face.

"What's her name? Does she want some chicken?"

The dark eyes studied me.

"Delilah," she said after a long pause. "I didn't name her. She was Grandmother Pam's doll in the olden days. I don't think she likes chicken much."

"Do you? I've got this extra piece I can't eat." I held it out and she took it politely, but I wasn't sure if she'd really eat it.

"My name is Constance," I said, aware that Murphy stood in the doorway watching us. Bobby and his bond mate were having some sort of heated conversation in whispers in a far corner. "But everyone calls me Stanzie for short."

"I'm Melinda," she said. "But everyone calls me Mindy."

"It's a nice day for a tea party, Mindy. It always seemed to rain whenever I wanted to have one outside when I was your age."

"You had tea parties?" Her eyebrows lifted a little bit as she considered this information. She took a bite of the chicken and chewed thoughtfully.

"Lots of them. I had a real china tea set. From Grandmother Elaine. My mother always thought I would break it but I never did. I was careful."

Understanding resentment flashed across Mindy's face. "That's why I have this plastic set. I wanted a real one but Molly said no. Kevin said I could have one for Christmas but now he's dead so I guess I don't know if I'll get one."

I did not react, because she watched me intently waiting for me to say something to destroy the fragile rapport we'd built together. Although it was all right for her, she did not want me talking about her daddy.

"This plastic set is nice, though." I gave it an admiring smile. "I like Cinderella best. What about you?"

"Belle," she said. Her face turned shy. "You want some tea, Stanzie?"

"I would love some. I need to wash this chicken down with something and tea would be perfect."

She moved Delilah to a lounge chair, telling me she had finished her tea, anyway. Then she ceremoniously filled my purple cup with pretend tea.

From the doorway Murphy smiled then moved away. I saw him sit next to Molly and I wondered if she'd talk to him. She probably would. Murphy had a way with women.

Mindy and I drank our tea and she introduced me to her three dolls and two stuffed animals—a panda bear and an elephant. She finished the chicken and her face was so solemn and sad I wanted to pull her into my arms to rock her and tell her it would be all right. But I didn't. I admired the dolls and petted the panda bear.

"Mindy?" The voice was thin and upset. Mindy and I both turned our heads to see Molly holding onto the edge of the sliding glass door, her face wan and pinched. "Go wash your hands, lovebug, and ask Miss Jolene to pour you some milk. It's time for dinner."

"I ate some chicken." Mindy pointed to the evidence reposing on the napkin by her tea cup.

"Not enough. Now you mind me, do as I say." Molly's eyes were red rimmed from constant crying and she looked ready to collapse.

Murphy hovered in the background and I could tell by his worried expression that he was ready to catch her if she dropped.

Eyes downcast, as if she were being punished, Mindy slid back her lawn chair and escaped inside, throwing her mother one look as she went by. They were both careful not to touch.

When she was gone, Molly staggered out onto the terrace and I smelled the alcohol on her breath from seven feet away.

She blearily pulled out a chair and sat on one of Mindy's dolls. She didn't appear to notice.

"I don't know you," she said with a drunk's belligerence. She saw me holding the stuffed panda and reached across the table to snatch it from me. "Don't you touch my child's toys. I don't know you."

"My name is Constance," I said in a low voice. I sat very still.

"I don't give a rat's ass what your name is. You can't come in here and start talking to my child without me telling you it's okay. Where the hell'd you come from, anyway?" Molly worked herself up into a fine frenzy. Murphy and Bobby Jenkins stood talking near the dining room table. Bobby's face flushed but he did not come outside.

I gave her the ridiculous story about how Murphy and I were newly bonded and looking for a pack. I wondered if she'd buy it any better than Bobby Jenkins had.

"Y'all don't want to join this pack. We let people drown in this pack. And y'all better not have been talking shit to my daughter about being Pack. We aren't telling her about being Pack until she hits sixteen or so. That's the way Kevin wanted it, and that's the way it's gonna be!" Molly glared defiantly at me. She also directed a black, scorching look into the house, straight at Bobby Jenkins. Which of us she was really talking to?

"I said nothing to her about being Pack. We talked about her tea set and her dolls." I looked across the table at her. Her whole body drooped with grief and misery, but her eyes were angry.

We stared at each other woman to woman, Pack to Pack.

"I lost my bond mates in a car crash two years ago," I said.

She gave me a startled look, drew in her breath with a gasping choke and burst into tears.

When Murphy and Bobby Jenkins came out onto the terrace, Molly and I were hugging each other. She sobbed into my shoulder as I rubbed her back. She was all bones and sinew in my arms. There wasn't much to her and I suspected most of her had drowned in that hot tub two nights ago.

"Hot damn," whispered Bobby Jenkins. "She wouldn't let us near her, but you walk in the door and ten minutes later she's crying like a baby in your arms." He looked suspiciously at Murphy. "Who the hell are you two? I ain't dumb. You're from the Great Council, aren't you? Trained in how to interrogate people. We didn't drown Kevin. How the hell many times do I have to say it?"

"We left him alone!" Molly lifted her tear-stained face to scream at him over my shoulder. "You, Jolene and me, we left him alone!"

Guilt oozed from her pores. I understood. They'd been having a threesome. Kevin was the odd man out and had gone into the hot tub to wait? Console himself? Usually Pack were not jealous of the occasional liaisons with other members. Mostly they did it because they wanted to shift. Sometimes a bond mate didn't want to shift, or there was a triad with an odd person out. Sex between pack members was common, although there were some who never strayed outside their bonds.

"He was a grown man, Molly, and he wasn't drunk when we went off together. He must have done that when we were shifted. I don't know what to tell you, honey. It was just a bad, bad accident. It's nobody fault." Bobby's voice got gentle and soft, and I moved aside so Molly could go to him. She did.

They embraced each other tightly—like pack. Tears gleamed in Bobby's eyes.

Jolene came to the doorway, a glass of milk in her hand. The little girl, Mindy, clung to her legs, peering out from behind her.

Murphy and I left when other members of the pack showed up. It wasn't a large pack—fourteen members, not counting the children. Bobby and Jolene's living room could only hold so many bodies and we weren't exactly welcome. We were tolerated.

Close to midnight, Murphy and I got into the gold Chevy Lumina he'd rented at the airport and drove back to our hotel.

"I can't see where this wasn't an accident, can you?" Murphy fiddled with the knobs of the air-conditioning. I wanted the windows down so I could feel the wind in my face. My wolf was fading, but still there and she loved the wind in her face.

"Was there an autopsy? Tox screens on his blood?" I put my window up with a sigh.

"Nothing," he said. "There was nothing. Interestingly enough, though, his blood alcohol content wasn't that high. Over the legal limit, but not by much."

"I fell asleep in the tub once," I mused. "My head actually went under the water. I woke up in a big damn hurry."

"Had you been drinking?" Murphy's face was pensive, washed pale by the oncoming headlights of the other cars on the freeway.

I shrugged. "Not much, but yeah."

"You're good with people, you know that?" Murphy gave me a sideways glance and I flushed. "That little girl opened right up to you like a flower and you helped her mother. You got her to a place where her pack could reach her. That was a good thing you did. Stanzie."

My nickname on his lips sent a small shiver down my spine. It made me want something more than I knew he could give me.

"Maybe I make up in this form what I lack in wolf form." He heard the bitterness in my voice and winced.

"No, what you are in wolf form is very much like what you are in this one," he argued softly. "You open people and wolves up. We drop our defenses around you, Constance."

I shrugged, not entirely convinced this was true.

"They aren't telling that little girl what she really is until she's sixteen. I don't like that idea, Murphy. A lot of packs are doing it this way now and I don't understand."

"Protection," Murphy said, but he was playing devil's advocate. I didn't think he much liked the idea, either. "They want their children to go to public schools, to make friends with Others. To not be so isolated and apart. It helps, they say, to build networks and resources so the children grow up and get good jobs and bring money and good things into the pack. Little kids talk. They would tell their friends about what we are."

"And how can it be proved even if they did?" I scoffed. "Nobody in the pack would obligingly corroborate the story. They'd pass it off as vivid imagination."

"Is that what your pack did with you?" he wondered and I flushed again.

"I was home schooled," I muttered, shifting around in my seat. "I don't have Others for friends."

"Do you have any friends, Constance?" He looked at me across the dashboard lights and I shrugged again. I was hurt but not surprised he didn't include himself as a friend. Only he was. He ought to have known that from when we shifted. Of course maybe he didn't want to be a friend.

"Your bite is bleeding again," I said to fill the strange silence. It was. I could smell the blood beneath the bandages. He'd worn a long-sleeved shirt to cover the bandage and it was dark so I couldn't see if the blood had seeped into the fabric.

He rotated his shoulder with a grimace.

"The grandmother in Paris wanted to give me stitches, but I wouldn't let her."

I blinked at him.

"You'll scar." I was horrified. "You'll scar and everyone will know that I bit you. I said I was sorry." I could not believe he would humiliate me like this. How could my wolf be so wrong about him?

"I wanted the reminder," he remarked. "It has nothing to do with humiliating you, Constance. Jesus, why do you take everything so damn personally?"

"Suffer then. Bleed all over the place. Whatever." I pressed my flushed face to the window and wished like hell I wasn't trapped in a car with him.

We remained huffily silent as we hurtled down the freeway.

"Reminder of what?" I asked when I couldn't take it any longer.

At first I wasn't sure if he were going to answer, but then he said, "Remind me that my way isn't the only way, and that I need to always try to see it from the other side, so I won't forget that there is one."

I bit my lip and took a deep breath. I could smell the air-conditioning, the ghost of a McDonald's meal past, fake new car smell and Murphy's blood. Among other things.

"Murphy? Are we friends?" I watched the big truck next to us flash by, going at least eighty miles an hour. Tiny red running lights winked and flashed, the noise of the engine deafening until it was past.

"Yeah, Constance," he answered in a voice so soft I had to strain to hear him. "I meant other people. I thought I was a given."

"Oh," I said, swallowing. It was hard because something blocked my throat. "Then, no. No, I don't have any friends."

That admission was difficult to make, because it made me sound pathetic, but at least I knew my wolf wasn't wrong, after all.

His gaze was fixed on the road ahead of us, but his fingers got very tight around the wheel. "I'm going to find us a pack. When this is all over, I'm going to find us a pack, Constance, and you're going to have lots of friends. Believe me?"

I nodded because I did.

"Will I have to shift with them at first? I mean, can I wait until you teach me what I need to know?" My heart hammered uncomfortably in my chest. "I'm afraid to shift with anybody but you, Murphy."

He sighed. I kept my head bowed, gaze fixed on my hands locked together in my lap.

"You see, this is exactly why I need a reminder. Because now you're scared you're not good enough, and I never wanted that. Didn't you say shifting brought you the most joy you ever felt anywhere, anytime?"

"Yeah."

"And I've taken that away. I'm sorry, Stanzie. Please forgive me. I had no right."

"You're just trying to help me, Murphy. Ever since we met that's what you've been doing. I'm sorry if I've been a bitch about it."

"You're as good as any damn member of Mac Tíre, or any pack anywhere. You tell me you understand that. Please tell me you do."

I half-smiled and wished I could. Something was wrong with me, or I wouldn't be the outcast I'd become. Murphy would help me and I wouldn't stay an outcast. I just needed to work hard and I could fix my shortcomings. I wouldn't be leaving a part of me behind as much as I would be evolving into the next stage. My wolf would still be my wolf, even when she could think in full sentences and knew how to follow and behave. There would still be joy left. My wolf was strong and not as easily bruised as I was. I had faith in her and Murphy.

I wanted tactile contact with him, but he always shied away from my touches. He needed to reach out first. I understood that even as I wished it were different.

In bed at the hotel, he curled up behind me, his arm around my waist. I felt his breath on my shoulder and I smiled as I closed my eyes.

* * * *

Even though we hadn't gone to bed until nearly two in the morning, I was wide awake at four AM. Murphy was sound asleep beside me, breathing deeply, his arm still around me.

I didn't want to disturb him, so I forced my eyes shut and managed to fall back to sleep.

But at seven AM it was no use. I could not sleep anymore.

Murphy was like a log and didn't even flutter his eyelids when I carefully dislodged his arm and got up to take a shower.

He opened one groggy eye as I put on my shoes—a pair of incredible brown suede ankle boots with zips up the back. One of my Paris purchases.

"You want to order room service for breakfast or go out?" I wondered, hoping for the latter. I felt cooped up and confined. My wolf was fading out fast, but there was still the whisper of her inside me, and I thought if I could get out into fresh air, she might blow away and go silent.

"Neither. I want to sleep. I'm wiped out, Constance. Goddamn jet lag." Murphy groaned. Sleep intensified his Irish brogue so I had to concentrate to understand him. The fact he talked into his pillow didn't help, either. "Take the car and go shopping, why don't you? I'll be up when you get back. Try to stay out for at least four hours."

I wanted to throw a pillow at his head, but when I turned around he was already asleep.

"I don't drive cars," I announced, but of course he didn't hear.

The desk clerk told me if I wanted to shop I needed to go to the Galleria, and he found me a cab and told the driver where I wanted to go.

The cab was a mini-van with the middle seats taken out. It was something of an ordeal to climb inside. The cab smelled of cheap pine air freshener with deeper undertones of underarm odor, as the driver obviously did not believe in deodorant. He spent most of the ride talking on his cellphone in a different language. Nigerian maybe? I couldn't tell. He drove like a maniac, weaving in and out of traffic, and barely kept one let alone both hands on the wheel.

I bounced and lurched around on the backseat, grabbing for handholds more than once, but I steadfastly refused to fasten my seatbelt. Murphy would have strangled me, but since I wanted to strangle him for not coming out with me, I figured we were even.

The cab screeched to a halt next to what looked like the entrance to an underground parking garage, and the driver took an inordinate amount of time hunting for his credit card machine. He asked me at least five times if I didn't want to pay in cash, and at least five times I told him I would love to do just that only there was one little problem—I didn't have any. Murphy had exchanged money at the airport, but I hadn't thought to take cash out of an ATM thanks to Mr. Jet Lag. I did have plastic and the signs plastered in the cab windows declared the driver took Visa, Mastercard and Discover, so I really could not see what the problem was.

After ten minutes of this bullshit, he swiped my card then I had to struggle with the damn van door, which slid closed but was extremely uncooperative.

I made a mental note to try to find a bus route back to the hotel and looked around to find a street entrance to the mall so I didn't have to descend into an underground parking lot and dodge traffic while trying to find my way inside.

This accomplished, I discovered that while I did not like Houston's cabs, I did like the Galleria. For one thing there were lots of shoe stores. Although I tried on about twenty different pairs, I didn't buy any. I did get Murphy a shirt in the Armani store. He'd bled on the one he'd worn yesterday and it was mostly my fault, so I figured I owed him.

One damn blue-and-white pin-striped shirt with a pocket cost me more than two hundred and fifty dollars. Decadent. Wicked. But then I thought of my eight hundred-euro Louboutins and forked over my credit card.

There was a huge ice rink on the bottom floor of the mall. Little kids and their parents skated and I stood on the floor above, and leaned over the railing to watch them. One chubby little boy fell a grand total of six times in forty seconds, but would not let his father hold his hand. Little kids made me laugh. They wanted to do it themselves. I could get behind that.

I wolfed down a chicken Caesar salad at La Madeleine and sucked down a bottle of Perrier. I people-watched while I ate and was disappointed, because I didn't see even one man wearing a Stetson. I thought everyone wore them in Texas. I did see lots of ball caps and t-shirts with sports team logos, but that's everywhere in America.

Somewhat let down, I browsed through the Tiffany store where I nearly bought a silver charm bracelet but told myself not to go overboard and walked out with nothing.

Half the time I was shopping I had to stop myself from turning to Murphy to share a joke or an observation. I wanted to see his sardonic smile and even his damn Red Wing boots.

If I'd known his shoe size I would have bought him a pair of *not* Red Wing boots, but I didn't so I had to content myself with the shirt. I guessed on that, but the salesman in the Armani store had the same height and basic build as Murphy and he'd told me his size, so I hoped it would fit. Besides, if it didn't, it provided an excuse to get Murphy back here to exchange it. Then I could buy him some new damn shoes.

Shopped out and dreading the idea of a cab, I tried to find a bus, but I had no idea what route I needed to take. In the end I found a cab that cruised by as I stood indecisively by the bus stop.

This driver at least kept both hands on the wheel, but the cab was old and squeaky, and even the hint of a bump sent me flying in the air. I vowed I would never take another cab in Houston again.

The lobby smelled like roses and floor polish when I walked in. The big-haired front desk clerk wore gray pants and a tailored white blouse, and she flashed me a white, toothy smile as I headed for the elevators. I could tell she wanted to ask me about Murphy—I suspected she had a crush on him—but luckily the elevator dinged and the door opened before she had the chance.

The *Do Not Disturb* sign still hung off the knob of the door to our suite. I checked my watch and shook my head, because it was after two in the afternoon. Lazy bastard.

But I cheered myself up with the thought that an afternoon "nap" didn't sound half bad. There were definite perks to being bonded, that was for sure.

I smelled it the moment I walked in. Sickness. Pain. A putrid scent of something gone very bad. The bag with Murphy's Armani shirt slipped out of my fingers and onto the floor. I barely noticed.

"Murphy?" My voice shook and I almost couldn't walk across the rug to the bedroom door. It was still closed.

When I opened the door and switched on the lights, the smell was twenty times worse. I could smell blood now and sweat, and faintly pulsing underneath it all—fear.

"Murphy!"

He was curled in a fetal position on the bed, shivering, yet his hair was drenched with sweat and the sheets beneath him were soaked.

Adrenalin slammed into my body, rendering me paralyzed at first, but the paralysis broke and I flew to the bed.

"Liam, talk to me!" I reached out to touch him. He was on fire he was so hot.

"Constance?" His voice was so weak, yet it had the power to rob me of the ability to breathe. "I...I...don't feel very well. C-c-can I have some water?" He slurred his words so I could barely understand him.

"Water," I whispered, horrified. I didn't want to leave him to find water, but I could see how dry his lips were. His eyes were dilated, even though the room was bright with the light of both bedside lamps. I got off the bed and couldn't remember for a moment what he wanted or what I was supposed to be doing.

"Please." He groaned, galvanizing me into action.

I ran to the mini refrigerator and got a cold bottle of water.

I had to hold the bottle to his lips, because he couldn't even sit up let alone hold it. He was disoriented and strangely apathetic. I supported him with my free arm and he was so hot and sweaty I didn't know how he could stand it.

I saw his eyes again and narrowed mine. My knowledge of herbs and home remedies awoke a deep suspicion—one that absolutely terrified me.

"What did you take?" I demanded as water dribbled out of the corners of his mouth. I took the bottle away and he slumped against my arm, his eyes fluttering wildly. "Tell me what you took, Murphy. Some kind of narcotic, right? You took something. Your eyes are dilated, you're slurring your words, come on, tell me, goddamnit!"

"N-nothing." He tried to focus on me but he couldn't quite do it. "J-j-just what the gran-grandmother gave...me."

I went rigid.

"What did she give you? Where's the bottle? Is there anything left?" I shook him and he groaned again. I felt like shit for doing it but I had to know.

"Duh-dresser." He tried to point but couldn't even lift his goddamn arm.

I knocked half the shit on the dresser onto the floor before I found a bottle of aspirin, and when I opened it and shook the pills out onto my trembling hand, there was a homemade capsule in among the manufactured ones. I recognized it as of the same kind we'd used in the herbal class at the Great Gathering.

I held my breath as I unscrewed the two halves and spilled the powder contained within into my palm. A tiny taste of it told me next to nothing. I scraped as much powder back into the capsule as I could and looked back at Murphy.

He lay very still and white on the bed and I didn't see his chest moving.

"Oh my god," I whimpered and I ran back to him.

He was still breathing. When I touched him, he grabbed my hand with both of his and opened his eyes.

"Stanzie," he said, his eyes very wide, and in my head I saw Grey and Rudi die, and I thought I was watching him die too.

"Liam, no!" I burst into tears and he collapsed back against the pillows.

"Gran-grandmother made a mistake?" he asked and my mouth dropped open as it all came clear to me. It was as if someone had given me a pair of glasses and the whole damn world had come sharply into focus. What was once blurry was now so clear.

"You're not going to do this, Murphy, you hear me." I tore my hand from his and threw myself on the floor to retrieve his cellphone—one of the things I'd knocked off the dresser.

I found Allerton's contact information and hit *talk*.

Amy Lee Burgess

I listened to it ring, hoping like hell this was his private line and that he answered it not some goddamned lackey.

Just when I thought it was going into voicemail, which would have been worse than a lackey, Allerton came on the line, and said, "Liam?"

"No, it's me. It's Constance." I sobbed. "Oh, you've got to help us. You've got to help him. I think he's dying, Councilor, and they'll blame me, I know they will, or the tox screen will be inconclusive only I've got one, I've got one of the pills, but I touched it and it has my fingerprints and they'll say it was me, because I know herbology, only this isn't an herb. It's some kind of narcotic. Maybe a pain killer, but it's way, way too much. He's overdosed and it's on purpose, because they don't want us investigating. They don't want us to know the truth!"

"Constance!" Allerton's voice was loud and commanding in my ear. "Stop talking now and listen to me. Where are you?"

"At the Magnolia Hotel in Houston." I choked. I looked back at Murphy on the bed and he wasn't moving, but his eyes were open. I couldn't move. I was paralyzed on the floor with the phone stuck to my ear.

"If someone is not at your door within ten minutes, you need to call nine-one-one. You need to call nine-one-one now if he's not breathing. Is he breathing? Is he conscious?"

Somehow I moved. Murphy was breathing, but barely. I touched his face and he took my hand and this time I didn't pull it away.

"If at any point he stops breathing, you call nine-one-one. Do you know CPR?"

"Yes."

"Good. I'm going to hang up now, but I'm going to call back in one minute when I've arranged things. Do you understand? Call nine-one-one if he stops breathing."

"I understand."

The phone went dead.

Murphy squeezed my hand and his eyes went very wide and dark.

"Sorcha!" he whispered.

"Murphy, it's me, Stanzie," I whispered back, squeezing his hand. He jerked it away from me.

He cried out her name again, then something in Irish that I couldn't understand. But I understood enough to know he thought he talked to her and it killed me.

"Liam, lie back." I pushed his thrashing body into the pillows, and he was so weak he couldn't fight me. He lay there panting and sweating, tangled in the sheets, and I tried to straighten them as he whispered her name again and again.

Chapter 11

Hospital chairs sucked. Plastic and hopeless, they were incapable of offering comfort and instead increased suffering. It didn't help they were usually puke-green or garish orange.

After the mad rush to the hospital in the back of an ambulance with a paramedic working like hell over Murphy's inert and collapsed body, they stuck me in some damn waiting room with green and orange plastic chairs from hell, and a broken vending machine.

I lost track of time after two hours. I sat in a puke-green chair with my head in my hands and thought about the Armani shirt and how the stretcher with Murphy's body strapped to it had rolled over it on the way out the door.

If Murphy died, maybe he could be buried in the shirt—if it weren't ruined by the stretcher's wheels. Maybe they'd let me do that much.

The ghosts of Grey, Elena and now Rudi haunted me. I kept seeing them die on me. Elena's broken neck and vacant stare from the backseat of the Mustang. Grey trying so hard to tell me it was okay, blood running out of his mouth as he stared into my eyes and died. Rudi, clutching at my hand, slumped against the expensive gold-flecked wallpaper in the ballroom of a French chateau, saying my name before dying. And now Murphy, pushing my hands away and calling out for his dead bond mate.

I'd been shopping and he'd been dying. He'd tried to show me how to be a proper wolf and I'd bitten him, and because of that, he was dying.

These people, these beautiful, vibrant, wonderful people, gone. I'd have to pick up the broken pieces of myself and try to put them back together again. Only each time it happened, more pieces went missing, and I'd never be whole.

Although I knew I wasn't responsible for any of these deaths, they still weighed heavily on my conscience simply because I'd been there. It was the grandmothers and grandfathers—they were the ones responsible for all the deaths. It hadn't been an accident that the pill Murphy had swallowed had contained some sort of deadly narcotic. It had been placed there on purpose to kill him. Just as everyone else had been killed on purpose. But still I felt guilty—as if I were stained to the soul with some unspeakable evil and I would never come clean.

I was crying when I felt someone's strong arm go around my shoulders.

I lifted my face to see Councilor Jason Allerton through a haze of tears.

"Do you have it?" His voice was gentle.

I reached into my purse, which I had braced between my feet and withdrew the aspirin bottle. It contained only the homemade capsule.

"Don't let a grandmother run the tests," I whispered.

"I won't," he promised.

"The grandmothers and grandfathers, they don't like the modern Pack, where we're headed. Everyone who died had a good job in the mainstream. Jobs that needed networks of Others, that brought attention. Elena developed new computer games. One was about werewolves. They were just games. Grandfather Tobias looked over my car that day. He was a mechanic. He did something. To kill Elena, and he didn't care if Grey and I were killed too. A grandfather worked in Sorcha's lab, didn't he? Or a grandmother."

"A grandfather. He was a janitor. He found Sorcha's body," Allerton confirmed. He kept his arm around my shoulders and I was grateful for the contact.

"Rudi gave a lecture on something I couldn't even understand. But he was going to make his pack rich. And that little girl's father, the one who drowned in the hot tub. He didn't want to tell his daughter what she was until she was sixteen. So she could go to school with Others and build a network and be mainstream when she grew up. They don't want us to change. They say we're soft and losing our connection with the wolf inside. They say we use that side of ourselves as a hobby, a game, an escape. And maybe they're right, but killing us off, would we really go back to the old ways?"

"You'd be surprised what people do when they're scared enough. There's been a huge cultural shift in the last hundred and fifty years, Constance. Modern things, modern times. And they're old enough, most of them, to remember something different where most of us now are not."

"They lied about the tox screens and the autopsies. They must have put something in the water, in Rudi's water, and then lied or substituted the results."

"I watched his autopsy performed. But you're right. They could have tampered with the tox screen results. The water bottles were misplaced. No way to test now. But yes, Constance. You've proved what I've been afraid to face or suspect."

"They'll say I tampered with his medicine," I warned. "But I didn't."

"I believe you and I will protect you, Constance. My word as a Councilor." He gave my shoulders a squeeze and I took a deep breath.

"He's dead, isn't he? Nobody's come to talk to me, or tell me anything and it's been hours. He's dead and you made them wait so you could tell me, didn't you?" My fingers went to my pendant and found the smooth perfection of the pearl Murphy had chosen for me. "Can I see him? It won't be real for me until I see him."

Arm around my shoulders, Allerton walked me down a long hallway, past a nurse's station and two orderlies lounging by a staff room door. I smelled lilies and medicine and sickness.

I waited to smell death, the black, strangling stench of death, Murphy's death, and the last little bit of my wolf faded out of existence. I didn't think I'd ever bring her back again.

Allerton opened the door to the room and I braced myself. I didn't smell death, which confused me until I walked through the doorway and saw Murphy.

Allerton's arm slipped away from my shoulders and he gave me a little shove toward the bed where Murphy sat up, pale but very much alive.

"I close my eyes for five minutes and you go and figure everything out and don't even clue me in. That's damned selfish, Constance, don't you think?"

I couldn't even begin to describe how I felt. It was a rush of emotions, but joy was predominant.

"You're the selfish one, Liam Murphy." I didn't know whether to laugh or cry so I did a little bit of both. "Making me think you were dying. I ought to kill you for scaring me, you know that?"

"I keep telling these fools it's jet lag, but they tell me it was a huge overdose of oxycodone. Doctors think they know every damn thing."

A white-coated doctor with a nice smile and a very shiny stethoscope shook his head. He stood by Murphy's bed but I hadn't even noticed him.

I knew by his smell he was Pack.

"Severest case of jet lag I've ever treated." He held out his hand for me to shake. "I'm—"

"Just leaving I hope." Murphy snorted from the bed. "Can't you see I want to talk to my bond mate, doctor?"

"He's going to be fine, as you can plainly tell." The doctor gave me a smile as he walked briskly to the door and left. Allerton was already gone.

Murphy and I looked at each other.

"Are you gonna stand there staring, or will you come closer? You scared of me or something?" Murphy gave me one of his boyish grins and I went to the bed, uncertain if my legs would hold me up much longer.

I sat on the edge of the mattress but didn't touch him. I wanted to so much.

"You been crying, Newcastle?" Murphy's voice was gruff and I nodded.

"You know I'm a crybaby. I cry over every damn thing," I said and to prove it, I started to cry again.

Instead of hugging me, he patted my arm and something broke inside me.

I got up and went to the window. Seven stories below a freeway crowded with cars flowed in a loop around the city. Houston was so faceless. I couldn't wait to leave.

"Guess who called and offered us a place in his pack?" Murphy's voice was jovial but strained.

As I'd sat in a puke-green hospital chair crying my eyes out, he'd been talking on the phone. He'd had time for Allerton to tell him the score and for phone calls from Irish bastards with different colored eyes. And when I'd needed him to touch me, he patted me on the arm like he would a child.

I nurtured the spurt of anger, because it helped stop the tears.

"Your friend, Paddy," I said to the window.

"Your friend too, Constance, if you give him half a chance. What do you say? I get the hell out of this damn hospital bed and we'll go to Dublin and join Mac Tíre."

I didn't say anything. I started to get pissed at myself. I'd thought he was dead and he wasn't and I should be happy, two minutes ago I had been happy, but now I was absolutely miserable. The man had nearly died, he had IV lines running in and out of his veins and all I could think about was that I wanted him to hold me.

Oh, Constance, you're pathetic, I told myself.

"If you're worried about shifting, I told you, it'll be you and me until you feel comfortable with others around you. Paddy won't push anything, I swear, Constance." His voice was gentle but starting to fray.

I still didn't say anything. My reflection in the window was puffy. My eyes were red-rimmed, my hair a frigging mess and I saw the blatant lie of my pendant gleaming against the dark glass.

"Tell you what, I'll find us a small pack and then you don't have to worry at all. You can run and play all you like, Constance. That's better, isn't it? That's what you want?"

"Murphy," I said with an impatient, bitter sigh. "You're lying in that damn hospital bed because of me. Because I bit you. I cannot continue to be what I am. I have to grow, if I'm going to shift, I have to be more than I am right now. So don't tell me we'll join a small pack and I'll go around being the child anymore because I can't."

"I pushed you too hard, Constance. It's why you bit me, because I pushed too hard, too soon. And I'll never make that up to you, I know, but let me try at least." Murphy's gaze fixed upon me but I wouldn't turn around.

"It's not my birthday until August, but that's just a formality. That's when it will be official, so you'll have to wait a few months but it'll go fast." I unclasped my pendant and held it in my palm. Murphy did not need the chaos that was me in his life. He'd done me a favor and saved me from Ducharme, but I'd paid him back. I'd figured everything out and now I should get the hell out if his life and not put him through the wringer every damn time I got insecure.

"You want to sever the bond." His voice seemed to choke a little and I leaned my forehead against the glass.

"I don't know what to do," he said. "I don't know how to fix this, but, please, Stanzie. Don't leave me. Give me a chance. Just one? That's all I'm asking, and if you're not happy by your birthday, then we'll have this talk, but please not right now."

I shook my head. A few months would make no difference.

He pounded a fist into the mattress. "What are you going to do, Constance? Run back to Boston with your tail between your legs? After your birthday and you're free, are you going to go to Regionals to find another bond mate?" Reproach and anger scorched through in his tone and I continued to look out of the hospital window rather than at him.

"I'm not going to go to Regionals, but I am going to go back to Boston," I admitted.

"Oh, for fuck's sake," exploded Murphy behind me. "You're gonna turn your back on the Pack, is that it? Because you're scared? I don't understand you!"

"It seems to me the Pack turned its back on me long before I turned mine on it." I put one palm flat against the glass. It was cold because of the air-conditioning and felt almost slimy beneath my skin. "I loved that old man, Grandfather Tobias. I used to visit him at least twice a week and have coffee in his little kitchen and listen to his tales of the old days when he was young and had a bond mate. I used to tell him things about my life and my bond mates and I loved him."

Behind me, Murphy sat up straighter in bed and gave me his full attention. I saw his handsome face in the glass of the window, totally consumed with what I told him. I had no idea why all this stuff spewed out of me, but it was as if I were a bottle of champagne someone had shaken then uncorked. I spilled and fizzed everywhere, unable to contain any of my buried resentment and my betrayal and rage.

"He was the first person I wanted to show my new car. I actually drove that car to him and asked him to take a look at it, because I trusted him and I wanted his approval. And he pretended to be happy for me and joked around with me and went underneath the car to inspect it and he did something, Murphy. He set me up. He wanted to kill Elena, but didn't care who he used to do it, and he used me, the one person in the whole pack who actually loved him and didn't think he was a duty or a burden. He didn't care if I died too, or that I would always bear the weight of knowing I was driving when my bond mates died. He cared more about the Pack than he did about me."

In my mind's eye I saw Grey and Elena as they had been that last, final night. Grey's hair pulled back in a ponytail. Elena's white dress. My fists clenched at the unfairness of it. I saw Grandfather Tobias and his crinkled, lopsided grin. I could taste the coffee he used to make for us to drink on Saturday mornings.

"He turned against me after the accident. He wouldn't answer the door when I went to him, when I wanted him to comfort me. He was the only one I wanted near me and he wouldn't answer the door. That's when I gave up, Murphy. When I started to think I was guilty and I did kill them. I wanted Grandfather Tobias to tell me it was a freak accident and not my fault, and he wouldn't answer the door. And the irony of the whole thing is he was the one who really killed them."

"His concept of the Pack, Stanzie, was skewed."

"Was it?" I whirled around. "We are a bunch of weak, posturing children. We don't live by our wits, and our wolves are pastimes and playthings, nobody knows that better than me. Somewhere along the line we've lost our pride, our honor. There are actually packs out there who don't tell their children what they really are because they're ashamed. They rationalize their decision and pretty it up so they don't actually say what they mean, but they are. They are ashamed! Grandfather Tobias was ashamed of me and you are too. Just let me go, Murphy. Let me go live in Boston and not be Pack anymore. I don't deserve it and I don't want it."

"I was never ashamed of you," he told me.

"Bullshit!" I shouted. "You liar! I saw your face after the first time we shifted. I heard what you said about how a bigger pack would never have let me get away with what I am. I'm a disgrace and I thought I could change, but I don't know if I can. What is the point? Everyone dies or goes away, and what is the point?"

"I didn't die. I'm not going to go away, not if you don't shut me out, Constance." Murphy's eyes were very dark as he stared at me.

"You? You're the worst one of all," I snarled. "When we're in bed together you won't even look me in the eye, and when I try to touch you,

you always shy away. I was right there with you, holding your hands, and you pushed me away and started talking to her. I'm not dead, but if I'm with you I'll have to live in the shadow of a dead woman, and I thought I could do it but I can't. I can't. I am tired of the dead having more power over me than the living. I'm tired of living in their shadows. You can work with me and help me and I could become a better wolf, a better person, but I will never be her and that's not how I want to live my life, Murphy."

He stared at me. "What did I say?" It was my turn to stare.

I had my arms wrapped around myself, because I was cold and wanted to be sick and it felt as if I were falling apart.

"When?" I gaped at him.

"To Sorcha. When I pushed you away and talked to her, what did I say?"

"I don't know. You were speaking Irish or Gaelic or whatever the hell language you speak. How the hell do I know what you said?"

He shook his head.

"So I'm being condemned by my words when you can't even tell me what I said, because you don't understand the language? That's harsh, Constance. You're going to walk away from it all because of something I said that you didn't even understand."

"I didn't have to understand. You're always talking to her. You say her name before you come, Murphy. You think my eyes are closed, but they're not. "

He bit his lip. "She was the only one I ever slept with until you. I'll admit the first time we went to bed I felt overwhelmed and guilty. I couldn't help it. I'm sorry for that."

My lungs could not seem to suck down a decent amount of air.

"Tell you the truth, Constance, I don't think I could have actually gone through with it with Sharon or Karen or whoever the hell she was at the Great Hunt. I just wanted to be alive again, that's all. I came to that Gathering and I realized how I'd been hiding and refusing to live without Sorcha. You think you were betrayed by your Grandfather Tobias, well, who the hell do you think got Grandfather Mick that job as a janitor? So he could watch over Sorcha, because the woman would work late nights, even when I pleaded with her not to." He shook his head, eyes dark with futile memory.

"She was so into her test tubes and experiments. She was going to save the planet, cure cancer, give something back to the world she took such delight in. And I couldn't be there so I asked Grandfather Mick, and now I find out he's the one who rigged the lights and that damned box. And maybe he even heard her fall and let her lie there dying and he did that for the Pack. For his Pack. But I don't want to creep back to Belfast and grow vegetables, Constance. I want to fight back. For my Pack, for the Pack that exists now, because we can't go back in time to a past that doesn't exist anymore. I wish you'd come with me and help me. I don't want to be alone anymore. And I know I pull away sometimes, but if I promise to work on that, won't you please try? Until your birthday?"

My mouth twisted but I didn't move.

"You want to know what I said to her? Because she stood there in that room, plain as day. She wore that green dress I loved so much and her hair was red as fire. She held her arms out to me and told me to come with her, that she had things to show me and somewhere warm and beautiful to bring me and all I had to do was take her hands. You know what I said?" Murphy's face was far off and dreamy. A small, bittersweet smile curled his lips. He laughed a little under his breath and then looked at me, all dreaminess vanishing.

My voice was a croak. "What did you say?"

"I said no, Constance. I said I wasn't ready, I didn't want to go. I wanted to stay. Then she was gone and you were there, crying, and I wanted to tell you to stop, but I couldn't make the words come. I don't remember much after that."

Taking a deep breath, I buried my face in my hands.

"It's all going so fast, Murphy. Two weeks ago, I didn't even know you and now you're my bond mate."

His smile was sympathetic. "I know. That damned Allerton loves arranging other people's lives, doesn't he?"

I laughed weakly. "He's a Councilor. They think they're elite or something. Powerful."

He laughed too but his eyes were suspiciously shiny. "Please put your pendant back on. At least until August."

With trembling fingers, I fastened the clasp around my throat, and for some absurd reason, felt immediately better.

Murphy grinned at me. There were dark circles under his eyes and he looked so very tired.

I was appalled at myself. "My timing has always sucked. I'm sorry, Murphy."

"I like your timing." He patted the bed beside him and I walked over and sat. I started to cry again like a complete idiot, and he handed me a wad of tissues from the box on the nightstand.

Blowing my nose helped me compose myself a little bit.

"What did you tell O'Reilly? Did you tell him we'd join the pack?" I asked and he rolled his eyes.

"I told him to go fuck himself, is what I told him." He laughed, and a small giggle escaped me despite myself. "But he said he'd call me back. Do you really think I'd have given him the satisfaction of accepting his offer without making him beg? Not to mention I don't make the decisions unilaterally for us. I'll not be rejoining that pack unless you want to as well."

He watched me toss the tissues into the wastebasket. "Do you?"

I shrugged, because I didn't know. I couldn't think of a pack without thinking of shifting, and that brought on a host of clamorous emotions I had trouble sorting out. I thought of my wolf, the way she loved to run, and my face twisted.

"Oh, Jaysus, I really did fuck everything up, didn't I? Stanzie, I'm so sorry." He sounded so disgusted with himself, and I wished he would touch me but he didn't. Of course he didn't.

Then it occurred to me that he was waiting for me to touch him, and I envisioned this huge stalemate where the both of us would walk around for eternity wishing the other one would reach out first and neither of us having the pride or guts to do it.

"What bullshit," I muttered, and before I could stop myself, I placed a hand on one of his.

We both stopped breathing for a moment then he hugged me, carefully, because of the IV drips in his poor, bruised up, bitten arm and it got much, much easier to breathe.

"I want you to make O'Reilly beg," I told him, and a cheerful grin split his tired face. I sat up straight on the bed but kept hold of his hand. "But

I do want to join the pack, Murphy. It's only the biggest, most prestigious pack in the whole world, isn't it?"

"One of them." He winked.

"I figure if I can interact as a wolf with Mac Tíre, fuck the rest of the Pack and what they think, I'm not the problem. But you'll have to help me, and that means making me interact with them and not letting me hide behind you. Because that's what I'll want to do and you can't let me no matter how much I whine and cry, okay? You promise, Murphy?"

He grinned. "I promise, Stanzie. You're a brave woman. I just hope I'm half as much help as you think I will be."

"Make O'Reilly beg a lot," I said and we both started laughing.

"I sanction your decision," declared Councilor Jason Allerton from the doorway where he'd stood for the gods knew how long, damn him. "But I hope you won't make this a drawn-out affair. I have work for you two and you can't be my Advisors without a pack." He gave us a grin and we gaped at him.

"Advisors?" I said in the same way I would have said "Well done" if someone had offered me an overcooked steak. I preferred my meat on the raw side.

"It's a thought." Allerton mused. "I find myself short-staffed, and here the both of you are and I thought perhaps the idea would appeal."

"It's an honor you offer us to be sure," said Murphy with a noncommittal expression.

"But?" Allerton leaned against the doorjamb and waited as though he had infinite patience.

"I don't know how long you've been listening, but you need to understand I'm not a very...developed wolf." I drew in a deep breath.

"I'm well aware of what you're like, Constance," said Allerton. "Your former pack leader made sure to tell me all about what he perceived as your shortcomings in that area. And others." He looked amused. "And frankly I don't care. I'm not in the habit of being impressed by posturing, insecure martinets like Jonathan Archer. Besides, you'd be my Advisor in this form. We don't do a lot of Council business in wolf form. Whether you wanted to develop your wolf or not is a strictly personal decision and has no bearing on my offer."

"Well, of course it does. It should," I argued. Murphy shut his eyes and leaned back into his pillows. "If I'm that irresponsible in wolf form, why wouldn't it bleed out into this one?"

"I would call you many things, Constance, but irresponsible would not be one of them. If you can't see why I would want you to be an Advisor, maybe I'm wrong to offer."

I looked at Murphy but he was no help, the bastard, he kept his eyes shut.

"Okay, so maybe I'm not irresponsible. But I am impulsive," I contended and Murphy either coughed or laughed, and I had my suspicions which one it was. "I tend to rush in and don't always think things through at first. I thought Advisors were supposed to be calm and cool like that French Advisor, Angelique. People want to talk to her, they're drawn to her and want to tell her things, because they think she'll understand and she's sympathetic."

Murphy did laugh that time and I wanted to hit him, but I took the high road.

"Didn't she draw out that little girl and her mother yesterday," Murphy said over my shoulder to Allerton, but he talked to me. "Weren't they both confiding in her and trusting her and them not knowing her fifteen minutes. And look at me. I'm not exactly a trusting soul or an easy one and hasn't she got me begging her to stay with me, because I can't even think about what it would be like without her around anymore. And I haven't even known her two weeks. But no, she's not Advisor material. She's not at all like that French woman. No. I can't see it."

"Not to mention the fact she took one week to figure out something I've been puzzling out for five years," added Allerton with a twinkle in his eye. "No, you're right, Liam. She's not Advisor material."

"Oh, shut up." I groaned then froze, because I had just told a Councilor to shut up. He and Murphy stared at me. "You see! You see how impulsive I am and how I rush in! I just told you to shut up! Me! And you're a Councilor. This is just the sort of thing I'm likely to do at the worst possible time and—"

"That's why Liam will be there too to pick up anything you knock over," predicted Allerton.

"She's more likely to be picking up after me," Murphy growled but he grinned.

"We'd be together?" I hadn't thought about that.

"Maybe not every case, but most of the time I would say, yes, you would be. Especially at the start," said Allerton.

"Accidents and murder and all that grief and anger," I said, cold to think of it.

"You can't hide forever, Constance. And you'll be helping people, not hurting them. But it's up to you and you can't do anything for me until you have a pack. So why don't you think about it and let me know in a few weeks' time? How about that? I think you could do with some time to think and relax." Allerton smiled at me again.

Slowly, I nodded.

"I'll await your decision but don't feel rushed. I want you to be sure." Allerton gave us a cordial nod then left.

Murphy and I still held hands. I looked down at our linked fingers and it seemed as though there might be a chance that my future would not be as bleak as I'd feared.

"When do you get out of here?" I looked up to see him staring at our hands too. He gave mine a squeeze.

"I've got to stay the night, damn it all," he muttered.

I squeezed back. "Maybe you should get some sleep then. It's late I think. I lost track of time hours ago."

"It's about ten o'clock," he said. "I am tired. You must be too. Why don't you go back to the hotel and take a bath. Get some room service. I'll eat Jell-o and try not to puke all over myself."

"Murphy, I'm not going anywhere tonight. Especially if I get to see you eat Jell-o and puke."

"Constance, there's only this one bed and I'm barely fitting it in myself with all these goddamn tubes and wires."

"I'll sleep in a chair. I can sleep anywhere, Murphy, in any position. It's one of my lesser-known talents. I'd be glad to demonstrate only I think you're going to fall asleep way before me. If only to avoid the Jell-o."

Murphy brushed some hair out of my face and tucked it behind my ear. His gaze searched mine.

"How will they do it? How will they stop the grandmothers and grandfathers? It's all over the world." I swallowed thickly and he squeezed my shoulder.

"I imagine there will be a rash of quiet arrests and word'll go out. It's not going to be overnight, and there'll probably be more young, promising people who die before this all ends. But we know what we're up against now. We know who we're fighting. Thanks to you."

"Oh, hell, I think Allerton knew but he couldn't prove it. You and I were guinea pigs," I whispered.

Murphy clucked his tongue. "I had no idea I'd bonded with somebody so cynical." But when we looked at each other we both knew what I said could be true.

"What will they do with the grandmothers and grandfathers they go after? Will they put them to death?"

Murphy nodded slowly.

"Yeah, I would think so. Murder's against our law, Constance."

I squeezed my eyes shut against the images that wanted to appear to me. Images of Grandfather Tobias and his slanted smile, and the way his eyes would crinkle when he laughed. He used to laugh with me a lot.

"If I'd never brought that car over there for him to see..." I choked out.

"There would have been some other opportunity. Constance, you can't think like that. You can't possibly change anything, so don't go there."

I shook myself as if I'd been submerged in water. "Do you want to be an Advisor, Murphy?"

"Do you?"

"I asked first."

Murphy played with my hair as he considered. His touch was soothing. I tried not to think about what might have happened if I hadn't gotten back to the hotel in time, or if things had gone differently here at the hospital.

All I wanted was to go away with him, somewhere safe, somewhere far, but his answer made me understand that it would never happen.

"I think I do. Yeah." He gave my hair a gentle tug. "Now you tell me what you want, and don't even try to lie, because I'll smell it if you do."

"I guess we could give it a shot. It's not as if you sign in blood and can never, ever escape. It might be fun. Definitely interesting."

Murphy gave me a slow, approving smile. "We're going to do grand things together, Stanzie, you and me. Grand things. You wait and see."

I was just so grateful I had the chance.

We might have stared into each other's eyes forever like a couple of sappy teenagers if not for the nurse who bustled through the door wheeling a cart. She placed a covered tray before Murphy after giving him a simpering smile. Even beat up and half dead, Murphy attracted women like flowers attracted bees.

"Aha!" I lifted the cover with a flourish to reveal—Jell-o. Lime green and disgusting.

"Ladies first," said Murphy with a gallant gesture toward the spoon. I rolled my eyes before tasting a jiggling spoonful.

"Not bad," I lied. "Your turn."

"Suddenly, I'm feeling very tired. I can't even seem to keep me eyes open." He feigned sleep.

As I watched him, the taste of lime Jell-o coating my tongue, my heart gave a strange little flutter. I wondered, really wondered, what the future had in store for us. Whatever it was, I wanted it. For the first time in a long, long time, I looked forward to what was coming more than I yearned in futile desperation for the past. It was a good feeling.

Epilogue

Sun is warm. Warm on fur. Warm on me. Run. Run fast! Run so fast, legs blur, trees blur, world blurs. Friend! Friend is here. Hello, Friend. Smell good. Taste good. Run, Friend? Run with me? Friend roll on back. Friend trust. Me roll too. Grass on fur. Sun in eyes. Friend takes my throat. No bite me. Friend never bites. Me no bite. We run. We run fast. Me want to run forever with my Friend.

Meet the Author

I've been writing since I was ten years old, but this is my first published novel. Beneath the Skin was written in a feverish haze the first eleven days of November. I blame the fascinating subject of shape shifting. What would people do if they had this ability? Is there a spiritual, instinctive connection between human and animal and if there is, how can I kick-start the spark of self-awareness within them both? Where would it lead? I guess I will have to continue Stanzie's story to find out.

Turn the page for a special excerpt of Amy Lee Burgess's

Scratch the Surface

Something's rotten in the Riverglow pack.

Still learning more about each other as bond mates and adjusting to their new roles as Advisors to a Councilor, Constance Newcastle and Liam Murphy must deal with the ghosts of their past.

A quiet weekend in Boston is anything but that, when Constance comes face to face with the betrayal of those she considered the closest to her. Everyone has secrets, and wherever Constance goes, she has a knack for uncovering them. The only problem is that some secrets are deadly

On sale now!

Chapter 1

*Wind in my face. I happy! Friend with me! We look at strange water. No move now. Stuck. Put paw on it. Cold! Want to walk on strange water. I scared! Strange water make noise—*Crrrack! *Paw wet and cold. Friend has tongue out, Friend laugh. Friend look at strange water. I not understand. Water moves. But strange water does not move . Why? Why? Want word for strange water. Want know why it not move. Think! Think hard. Strange water there when it very cold. Me seen it with Him and Her before they go away and not come back. Us run on it. Run, run, run. Me not want run now, me want word. I. I want word. I want word for strange water. Think. Think. Friend watch over me. Think. Think. I so* mad. *I want word! I want word! No. No get mad. Can't think for mad in head. Go away, mad. Stop. Think. Strange water not move. Cold. White. Water. Not water. Think. Think. Want word. Word for strange, cold water that not move. Word is...word is...ice! Yes! Ice, ice, ice, ice! I see ice! I see ice! Friend, I see ice! Friend, I happy! I see ice! I lick Friend's face. Friend lick me. I happy. I see ice!*

* * * *

The shrill ring of the phone dragged me out of sleep. Murphy and I had shifted the night before and we'd exhausted ourselves in wolf form. By the time we'd shifted back, shivered into our clothes and driven home to Boston, it had nearly been dawn. The sky above my condo had been a pale shimmering pink as I'd fallen onto the bed, my hair still wet from the shower. I didn't even remember Murphy coming to bed but he was there with me. The ringing phone had roused him too. He was snuggled up against my back, his arm across my waist and he rolled over into a defensive ball, swearing colorfully in Irish under his breath while he tried to shield his ears with one of the fluffy down pillows.

"Goddamn it," I muttered. I could tell it was frigid outside. Well, naturally, it was January. Barely. "Happy fucking New Year, Murphy."

His only response was more Irish swearing. The phone stopped ringing and I let my eyes drift shut again but that's when the damn answering machine kicked on with an earsplitting beep.

"Fuck." Murphy's curse was muffled by the pillow.

"Constance," said someone familiar. We both scrambled up on our elbows, wildly shifted the covers and tried to get the phone before it disconnected.

Since the phone was closer to my side of the bed, I won the mad race and scooped it up, panting and out of breath.

"Hello, Councilor Allerton," I gasped into the phone while Murphy performed some sort of strange-looking war dance on the cold hardwood floors. I didn't feel much sympathy. I had told him to wear socks to bed and he had refused.

"Is there no frigging heat in his place?" He hopped from one foot to the other.

"Good morning, Constance, did I wake you?" Jason Allerton was a Councilor on the Great Pack's Council. The Council oversaw all of the packs spread out across the world. Murphy and I were his newest Advisors. He sent us on assignments to other packs to investigate accidents, murders and disputes that could not be worked out by the Regional Councils and other projects as he desired. So far, we'd only been on one assignment for him and that one had been unofficial, before we'd affiliated with Mac Tire—one of the largest, continuous packs in the world. They were based in Dublin, Ireland, but we had yet to go there. I'd only met two people from my new pack—Murphy and the Alpha male, Padraic O'Reilly. The rest were amorphous strangers I supposed I would eventually meet.

At the moment Murphy and I were in Boston, Massachusetts. I owned a condo and we were in the process of cleaning it, packing up the stuff I wanted to keep and getting it ready to act as rental property. When all this was accomplished, we would go to Belfast to clear out Murphy's cottage there before we went to Dublin to meet the rest of our pack.

After Councilor Allerton had asked us to be his Advisors, Murphy and I had been asked to join Mac Tire. In Murphy's case it was rejoin since he had been born into the pack and had left after the death of his bond mate, Sorcha, but it was a new pack for me.

Murphy had bought a car in Houston and we'd spent the past two months leisurely driving to the East Coast, stopping at all the major cities that interested us so we could sightsee. I'd seen more of my native country in the past two months than I had the previous thirty-two years of my life.

We'd arrived in Boston the day before New Year's Eve, so we'd barely even begun to tackle the condo. Murphy didn't want to be on a time table. He wanted us to go slowly and explore. I think he meant each other as well as the cities we visited. We'd been thrown together and bonded under extreme circumstances and now that the dust had settled and we were still standing, we had a lot of getting to know each other to do.

In the three months I'd known him, he'd rapidly become my best friend and confidante. My teacher and my guide.

After my first bond mates, Grey and Elena, had died in a car crash two and a half years ago, I'd been kicked out of my small pack in Connecticut. Although the Councils had cleared me, my pack had never stopped believing I had been drunk the night I drove that car over the embankment and my bond mates died.

It had been later proved that it was Grandfather Tobias, another member of my old pack, who had tampered with the brakes of my new Mustang. He was part of an underground movement made up of some of the oldest members of the Great Pack who resented the new ways we were adopting that brought us closer into interaction with the Others—those who were not Pack—and brought money and prestige into our packs by way of this involvement.

The new direction was integration, although not going as far as to reveal we were Pack and could shift into wolves. The old way was behind the scenes, on the fringes. Jobs in retail were common, but some of us were con artists or magicians as well. The trick was to avoid attention and interaction with the mainstream world as much as possible.

This movement saw to it that certain young Pack members, who flouted tradition, met with fatal accidents. It was meant to scare us, stop the flow of revenue and destroy the ones with the closest ties to the Others.

Murphy and I, with Councilor Allerton's assistance, had discovered and unmasked this movement. We had not stopped it because it could not be halted simply by announcing to the Pack it existed. That would have caused chaos and panic. They had to be stopped one and two at a time—quiet arrests and detainment.

We'd barely scratched the surface and I knew a lot of work was yet to be done, but after what we'd gone through in Paris and Houston, I wasn't sure I had the stomach for it.

This was the other reason for the long road trip—it was a chance to regroup and get myself together.

Allerton had checked in on us a few times along the way, but I wondered if this phone call heralded the end of the vacation and was a wake-up call in more than one sense of the word.

However, his next sentence blasted everything out of my mind.

"We've arrested Tobias Green and he's confessed."

Murphy stopped hopping and swearing when I pulled out the desk chair and fell into it. My legs felt hollow, as if all the bones had melted.

Tobias Green. I called him Grandfather Tobias. I'd loved and respected him. I'd looked after him more than anyone else in my pack and, although I'd had a sense of duty because he was old, I'd done it more out of genuine love. He was not my blood grandfather, but he might as well have been. I loved him that much.

Ever since that moment in Houston when I'd realized the grandmother in Paris had deliberately put a lethal overdose of narcotics in the homemade pill she'd given Murphy, it was an easy, yet devastating, intuitive jump to understand that Grandfather Tobias was guilty of killing my bond mates. Once we'd uncovered the grandmothers' and grandfathers' plot, it had been horrifyingly clear he'd done something to the car. I'd brought it to him that afternoon and he'd gone beneath it to inspect it because he was a mechanic and he told me he wanted to see for himself that his dear girl and her bond mates were in a safe, reliable vehicle. Yet he'd tampered with the brakes so they'd fail and I'd lose control.

Without being able to prevent it, I flashed back to the accident.

* * * *

"The Comet or Blue Moon, Grey? Which club do you want to go to?"

I see Grey laughing in the dashboard lights as he fiddles with the CD player. Depeche Mode's Strange Love morphs into Billy Idol's White Wedding. Grey has an addiction to eighties music. Sometimes I find it endearing. Sometimes I find it annoying as hell.

"I don't care. It's your birthday, Stanzie. You choose. The Comet or Blue Moon, it doesn't matter to me." He turns his head to smile at me. The love he feels for me is written all over his face. His shaggy, dark hair falls into his blue eyes. He's got the back part confined in a rubber band. When it's loose, his hair brushes his shoulders. Right now it's about two inches longer than mine. I'm experimenting with a bob. I'm not sure I like it.

He needs a haircut. He has an appointment on Monday. I wrote it on the erasable calendar stuck to our fridge. I made it for him yesterday.

"Elena?" I glance into the rearview mirror to see her beautiful face. She is putting on eyeliner and her bright red purse is open on the seat beside her—a compact in one hand, the eyeliner stick in the other. She frowns at her reflection, with concentration, not because she finds fault with her appearance.

"Oh, you know I don't care, I just want to dance with you, Birthday Girl."

The Comet is closer and I have a sudden desire to be out of the car. I want to feel the summer breeze and hear my new metallic gold stiletto heels click against the soft, warm pavement of the August night. I want to hear music from this decade. I want to dance, to feel Grey's hands on my hips as we move together beneath the strobe lights and Elena guards our drinks at the table.

I make a decision. I take the exit. The road climbs over a small crest then dips sharply. I brake because we've been traveling at seventy miles an hour and now we need to slow down. We'll still be above the legal speed limit, but this is a Mustang GT, metallic gold like my stiletto heels, with an ink-black leather interior. My dream car is a present from Elena who has just signed a lucrative contract with a company that develops PC games. Elena is a whiz at designing games. We have six different PCs and laptops set up in our house in New Britain and she is always perched in front of one of them, sucking absently on her bottom lip as she contemplates the scenarios in front of her on the screen.

Yesterday she made an important deliverable to the company and they extended her contract for another game, this one even more ambitious—about werewolves. It is slated for tentative release October of 2010, which is two years and two months into the future.

I put my foot on the brake, but it doesn't seem like we decelerate. Confused, I press harder then we hit the dip and I see a shadow or a bird or something that distracts me then the wheel is a traitor beneath my hands. Elena screams in the backseat as the guardrail looms closer.

I have time to think to myself, This is just a dream. This is not happening. This is not—

The Mustang's front end smashes into the guardrail with a terrific bang. It crumples with a metallic grinding and tearing. The engine screams in protest.

"Stanzie!" Elena shrieks. Grey is stiff and terrified beside me. The whole car reeks of our extreme fear. It pours out of our skins like invisible sweat and the mad stink of it paralyzes my muscles and vocal cords. I am a mute statue. I cannot even blink.

As Billy Idol sings the Mustang turns up and over. Wind rushes in when Grey's door flies open. I see a blur of movement when he falls out and my paralysis breaks. I reach out for him, but the airbag hits me in the face and something hard smashes the back of my seat. Elena stops screaming. She stops screaming because her neck breaks under the force of her body slamming into the back of my seat. She, like Grey, never wears a seatbelt.

* * * *

Pressure brought me out of my trance. Murphy squeezed my shoulder reassuringly.

Allerton said my name, probably not for the first time.

The car crash was so vivid in my head I could still hear Elena's screams and the jagged sound of tearing metal.

"I'm here." I swallowed an obstruction in my throat. It was two and a half years ago. It was time to let go and get over it.

I'd been doing a good job of that, thanks to Murphy, but one sentence made me realize that maybe I would never truly be free. It was not a pleasant thought.

"I'm sorry if I've upset you." Allerton's voice was rich with sympathy. I visualized his handsome, distinguished face and his dark black hair he wore as fashionably cut as his designer suits. "I thought you should know. There's something else as well."

My stomach sank even though I had no idea what the something else could be, only that it wouldn't be good.

"He wants to speak to you. Privately."

My mouth dropped open in protest. Sick bile burned my throat and I must have twisted in my seat because Murphy put both hands on my shoulders. I was absurdly grateful for his touch.

With his Pack-enhanced senses, he could hear what Allerton said, and he could smell my distress. I know I reeked of it.

"Do I have to?" Tears clogged my sinuses and, if not for Murphy, I would have been bawling like a baby, I knew it.

"Of course not," said Allerton at once, and there was just a tinge of disappointment in his voice that I strove to ignore, but it was impossible. Damn him. Damn me for wanting to please him because he was a Councilor.

"Where is he?"

"He's being held in the safe house in Hartford. I'm here with him, along with one of the Regional Councilors. Riverglow is not being told the whole story. Just that he confessed to doing it not why."

Riverglow was the name of my former pack—Jonathan, Nora, Callie, Vaughn and Peter.

"Aren't they even curious?" I couldn't disguise the bitterness in my voice.

"He's saying he accidentally put a hole in the brake lining, causing the brake fluid to leak out, and he realized it when he went over the car after the accident but was too ashamed to admit it."

"An accident? And do they believe it?" My voice shook with outrage. "They didn't believe me. Are they going to believe him?"

"Constance, he had to say something. We need to keep the knowledge that people in the Pack are murdering others under wraps. He can't tell them the truth." Allerton was sympathetic but firm. "And you can ask them yourself what they believe if you come to Connecticut. They want to see you too."

I wanted to throw the phone into the wall and stomp on it. I wanted to spit in Allerton's arrogant face. What I didn't want was to ever see any of my former pack again—especially Grandfather Tobias.

"How am I supposed to face them? How am I supposed to look Grandfather Tobias in the eye after what he did to Grey and Elena? To me!" It was disrespectful to say the least to shout at a Councilor, but I rarely paused to think before I reacted. Allerton took my tirade in patient silence which is what made me stop shouting. My cheeks burned with humiliation.

"I'm not telling you what to do, Constance. I'm giving you the opportunity to hear the man out. It might provide some closure." He didn't say it, but I knew damn well he thought I could use a huge, heaping dose of it.

I squeezed my eyes shut and heard Elena screaming in my head again.

"When do I have to be there?"

"As soon as you can make it." Allerton paused then said, "He's not going back to Riverglow. The Council will acknowledge his cover story and accept it, but he won't return to the pack. He's going to go to sleep one night very soon and he's not going to wake up. If you want, you can hand him a glass of warm milk or hot chocolate to help him go to sleep. If you want." Allerton's tone was deceptively nonchalant but what he offered was the chance to administer the fatal poison. That would be closure for sure.

I didn't answer because I couldn't. A part of me wanted to kill that old man, not with poison, but with my claws and fangs—in wolf form. I didn't know if I could be such a civilized murderer. Or maybe executioner was a better word.

"Can I speak to Liam, please?"

I thrust the phone at Murphy and he took it, but when I tried to get up, he frowned at me.

"I want to take a shower." I had to get out of the room and away from the phone and Allerton and the sound of Elena screaming.

His dark gaze searched my face for a moment before he let go of my shoulder. He watched me as I stumbled for the bathroom. He acknowledged Allerton then went grimly silent as he listened. I smelled the anger that escaped from his pores and clouded the air around him—protective anger.